A lone man, in over his head, against a corrupt town in the middle of nowhere.

Toby Sawyer starts the night with a simple job: babysit the body of Luke Jordan. Luke, one of a family of four brothers (all bad apples), has gone and got himself shot over what appears to be getting too friendly with someone else's girl.

Toby's working part time for the police department, hoping he'll someday get the bump up to full-time deputy. He's got a trailer, a wife, a baby boy, and not much else. Coyote Crossing isn't exactly a hotbed of opportunity for a young man, after all.

Unless, of course, a young man has a knack for the illegal. Turns out Luke Jordan might have been involved in smuggling Mexican illegals up through Texas. Turns out Luke Jordan might not be the only one in town with a stake in the operation. Turns out Luke Jordan's death might not be the last one on this hot Oklahoma night ...

The Deputy

by Victor Gischler

DISCARD

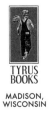

TYRUS
BOOKS

MADISON,
WISCONSIN

Published by
Tyrus Books
1213 N. Sherman Ave., #306
Madison, Wisconsin 53704
www.tyrusbooks.com

This book is a work of fiction.
Names, characters, businesses, organizations, places, events,
and incidents either are the product of the author's imagination or
are used fictitiously. Any resemblance to actual persons, living or dead,
events, or locales is entirely coincidental.

Printed in the United States of America
14 13 12 11 10   1 2 3 4 5 6 7 8 9

ISBN 9781935562009 (paperback)
ISBN 9781935562016 (hardcover

For Jackie

ACKNOWLEDGMENTS

Thanks big time to my whole family, especially my wife Jackie and son Emery who had to put up with a grumpy writer when things weren't going smoothly and a slightly silly writer when things were going well. First readers (and super cool pals) Anthony Neil Smith and Sean Doolittle will always get props. Video Golf on me next time, guys. Super-fly agent David Hale Smith derserves big thanks as does his right hand Shauyi. Hello to all my peeps back in Oklahoma. You didn't think I was done writing about Oklahoma, did you? And thank you, readers. And finally, I am grateful to Alison and Ben of Tyrus Books. You gave this novel a home. Much obliged.

CHAPTER ONE

I faked a cough, put my hand over my mouth to hide the grin. I knew it wasn't funny really, but the surprised look on Luke Jordan's dead face caught me just right. Luke was the first dead guy I'd ever seen up close except for in a funeral home.

Chief of Police Frank Krueger sighed out long and loud and scratched his big belly, pushed his straw hat back on his forehead, wiping the sweat off his face with a red handkerchief. He looked down at the body of Luke Jordan lying half-in half-out of the old pickup truck and began counting, stabbing his fat finger at the body. Finally he said, "I count nine bullet holes. That what you got?"

I didn't bother counting. "Yeah." I fingered the tin star pinned to my Weezer t-shirt, feeling stupid in untied high-top sneakers and sweatpants. When the chief phones you out of bed at midnight, you grab what you can and run out the door. I held the holstered revolver behind my back. I'd tried clipping the holster to the sweatpants, but the gun was too heavy, kept pulling the waistband down past my ass-crack.

So I didn't count the bullet holes, but I looked hard at Luke Jordan, eyes wide and surprised as hell, blood all gunky and black and starting to dry on his plaid shirt. Luke was one of these good looking rednecks in a rough way, all faded jeans and t-shirts with the sleeves ripped off. Cowboy boots, some kind of fake lizard skin. Probably told everybody they were rattlesnake.

In high school civics class, Luke used to chew up notebook paper until it was nice and soggy then fling it at the back of my head. After graduation, Luke's brothers had driven him down to Tulsa to see the Army recruiter. The Army had sent him back a month later. Luke said it was bad knees, but I'd heard somewhere they'd kicked him out for fighting and drunkenness. He'd been kicked out of gym class for pretty near the same thing.

Chief Krueger slapped a hammy hand on my back. "Stay here and watch the body, Toby. I'm going to talk to Wayne."

"Okay, Chief."

"Billy gets here you tell him he's on my shit list," Krueger said. "He only lives on over to Dixon. Should have been here ten minutes ago."

"Check."

The chief walked over to Wayne Dobbs who sat on the front steps of Skeeter's, the local watering hole and burger joint. It had been Wayne who'd found Luke's body, called the chief at home. You're allowed to call the chief of Police at home if you're on the town council, I guess. Wayne had been the late night cook and wash-up guy at Skeeter's for as long as I could remember, even kicked me out of the place when I was sixteen and trying to get beer on a fake I.D. Now he was the owner. Wayne had American dreamed himself to the top of the food chain. Hell, it sure was a small damn town.

Wayne stood when the chief came over, wiped his hands on his apron then started pointing and talking, and I knew he was telling the same story over again about hearing the shots and finding Luke's body.

The chief nodded, and they both walked into the bar.

I went to my rusted as shit Chevy Nova and opened the passenger door, leaned in and fished a pack of Winstons and a Bic lighter out of the glove compartment. I leaned against the hood and lit up, sucked the smoke in deep, then blew a long gray stream into the night.

The smoke clung, drifted, looking for a puff of wind to hitch a ride. But there was no breeze. Humid. It was hot, hot, hot fucking August in Oklahoma, and when the sun came up and cooked Luke Jordan's body for a while it would get awful ripe real quick.

I looked up and down Main Street. The road glistened a dead black, the brick buildings closed up and sleeping. The chief said he chased a few folks back inside before I'd arrived. Guess they'd heard the shots. Only a few folks lived over their stores like in the old days. The barber shop, dime store, bank all looked like a deserted movie set. The light at the four-way stop blinked a hellish red. God cued a cat somewhere to meow and knock over a garbage can.

Headlights flashed at the other end of Main. They came close, and I saw it was the other squad car, Billy Banks behind the wheel. He pulled in next to me and climbed out. He wore ironed khaki pants and shirt, black tie. Shoes polished. His gun belt hanging at a jaunty, gunslinger angle. Billy was all close black haircut and brushed teeth and trimmed finger nails. I thought he was running for some office, although God knows what out here at the ass-end of Oklahoma. Dog Catcher maybe.

He nodded at me. "Toby."

I grinned. "Chief says you're late."

Billy smiled back. "He in there talking to Wayne?"

"Yeah."

Billy squatted next to Luke, wrinkled up his face like he'd eaten some bad egg salad. "Jesus, Luke pissed off somebody bad, huh? I bet he got drunk and his hands got busy after the wrong girl. Half these good old boys around here got pistols under their car seats."

"Uh-huh." I kept smoking. It was too hot to keep up my end of the conversation.

Billy saw the chief coming and stood, straightened his tie. "Got here as quick as I could, Frank."

Krueger looked at his wristwatch then back at Billy. "Have yourself a cup of coffee? Read the morning paper?"

Billy smiled like it was a joke, but he knew it wasn't.

I dropped my cigarette, ground it into the dirt with my heel. Krueger motioned he wanted to have a pow-wow. We made a little huddle.

The chief thumbed a giant wad of tobacco into his mouth, cheek bulging. He chewed, spit, then said, "Wayne says Luke was talking to some Mexican gal an hour before closing."

Billy lifted an eyebrow at me, smile twitching into an *I told you so*. Yeah, you're a genius, dude.

"Probably had a boyfriend."

"He ever see the Mexican gal before?" Billy asked.

"Nope."

Chief Krueger blew his nose into the same red handkerchief he'd used earlier to wipe his forehead. That handkerchief got around. He was sweating pits under his arms and around his collar where his jowls hung over. The sun wasn't even up yet. Jesus. I hope I never get that fat. But the chief wasn't just fat. He was big. Like some kind of king grizzly bear. I'd seen him punch a man into the next county.

Chief punches a guy, and the guy stays punched. So no fat jokes coming from me. At least not out loud.

"You think his brothers know?" Billy asked.

"I thought of that," Krueger said. "Thought maybe I'd ride out there."

The Jordan brothers. Six of them—well, five now. The oldest brother Brett was doing a stretch for transporting crystal meth, but the others wouldn't take the news about their brother Luke too well. Matthew was like a big, dumb bull. Evan and Clay could be downright mean, and I knew for a fact the next oldest one, Jason, had killed a man with a meat cleaver. Got off for self defense.

I said, "Maybe just call, Chief. It's almost twenty miles out to their place."

He shook his head. "Some news you have to deliver in person." He spit tobacco, left a thin trail down his chin. "And I think I'd like to make sure their trucks are parked out there. If I call and there's no answer, they can say they didn't feel like getting out of bed."

I wasn't sure what he meant, but I didn't say nothing.

Krueger rubbed his chin. "I'll drive out there. Billy, I want you to open up the office and get the paperwork started. Toby, watch the body."

I blinked. "What?"

"Watch the body."

"He ain't going anywhere."

Krueger gave me a look that made me wilt. "Son, you can't leave a corpse lying in plain sight unattended. You're the part-time deputy, so you get the grunt work. You want to earn your way on full time, don't you?"

"Okay."

"Billy will get the paperwork started and leave a message for the county coroner. Lord knows how long it'll take that lazy son of a bitch to make it out our way. I won't be gone long." He looked at the holstered revolver in my hand. "Stick that under your car seat."

Billy gave me a wink and headed for the station.

The chief put a hand on my shoulder. "You know I have faith in you, boy."

"I know."

"I need you to grow up a little bit. We get you on the payroll full time, we need to show the other fellows that you're mustard. That you belong. Right?"

I nodded.

The chief had known my parents, knew my situation when I came back. Some of the folks around town had looked at the chief funny when he'd given me the tin star. Even if it was only part time. But nobody questioned him. He was the chief.

He was the Sheriff too. Town council gave him the chief job, but he had to get elected to be sheriff, and Krueger had won reelection four terms in a row. Paychecks for the deputies came out of the county fund, and the chief position was overseen by the city. Since Coyote Crossing was the only town in the county, I wasn't sure how it made a difference.

Anyway, the chief liked to be called chief, not sheriff.

Krueger gave my shoulder one more friendly squeeze.

He got into his squad car and drove off into the dusty wide nothing of Oklahoma. The darkness ate his taillights, and I stood with my shoe-laces untied, babysitting Luke Jordan's mortal remains.

About ten minutes and three cigarettes later and I'd had about enough of watching Luke's wide-open eyes, and it was hot anyway. I wondered why I had to watch the body. Couldn't we just bag it? And why didn't Krueger call the county boys? We'd never had a shooting inside the town limits before. On *Law & Order* some guy usually snapped a few pictures of the stiff, and I wondered if maybe Billy was coming back later with a camera. Maybe they'd let me take the pictures. That would be cool if I snagged the corpse photographer gig.

I left the body and went into Skeeter's. Wayne was pushing a pile of dust and bottle caps across the floor with a ragged broom. He looked at me. I waved, reached into the cooler and grabbed a Coke. "Pay you tomorrow, okay, Wayne?"

"Sure." But he didn't sound thrilled about it. Guys like that always worried on the details.

Wayne was on the town council and still swept up his own place every night. Coyote Crossing was that kind of town. Hell, if I ever got to be the boss of anything, be damned if I was still going to do the sweeping up. What was the point? Wayne was stooped. His bald head gleamed with sweat. Deep, dark eyes and an acne-scarred face. He worked so damn hard at everything, it seemed to me like he was always about to fall over.

I picked up the pay phone and dialed Billy at the station. He answered, and I asked, "Billy, how come the chief didn't call the county?"

He sighed big. "Let him worry about it. Just keep the flies off Jordan."

"You want anything before Wayne closes up?"

"No thanks."

"Okay." I hung up.

But instead of going back out to the body, I took down one of the stools Wayne had put up and perched there, sipping the Coke. I put the cold can against my forehead. I'd sure be glad when it got around October and cooled down some "Looks like Luke had trouble with some Mexicans."

"No Mexicans in here." Wayne didn't look up from his sweeping.

"Chief said he was grabbing ass with some Mexican girl."

"Oh." Sweep, sweep. "He told you, huh?"

"Sure. Why not?"

"Just didn't want to make a story out of it, I guess. The chief'll handle it."

"Yeah."

I put the stool back and took my Coke outside.

I went back to the body. Luke Jordan's eyes looked like wet glass, his skin like rubber or something. A body sort of looks fake when the life goes out of it. He looked like a fake dead body in a Shriner's haunted house fundraiser. I looked up and down the street. Nobody around. I knelt next to Luke, took the wallet out of his back pocket. No cash. Damn. I put the wallet back. I found a set of keys in his front pocket. The chief would probably ask me to move Luke's truck later, so I took them and put them in the glove compartment of the Nova.

I leaned against the Nova, sparked up another Winston. How long would this take? If I stood here all night, I might need to arrange some things. My wife Doris had to be at the diner for her shift by seven which meant somebody had to watch the boy if I couldn't be there. Maybe that old Indian woman we hired sometimes. She worked cheap.

Damn. I sure as hell needed the department to put me on full time, but Coyote Crossing sucked hind tit as far as the state budget was concerned. What pioneer dumbshit named this place Coyote Crossing? Some white guy probably. It probably used to be called some Creek Indian word that meant scorpion hell spirit bullshit or something, and then the railroad came through and some white guy changed it. I'd have to remember to look that up some time.

I had a long list in my head of things I wanted to look up. Some day. Not like I owned any encyclopedias. Maybe in the library.

I finished the cigarette, flicked away the butt and looked at my watch. I'd killed exactly ninety-seven seconds.

Hell.

Screw this.

I hiked the three blocks to Molly's house. Molly was about the only good thing in this town when I came back. I'd left with a guitar and six hundred bucks I'd saved up mowing lawns and pitching sod. Came back to bury my mother and got stuck. The town hadn't grown one inch since I'd been away. Hell, we were so far out you couldn't use cell phones. Satellites didn't fly over. We might as well have been in another fucking dimension. I'm surprised they bothered putting us on the road maps.

I thought about getting a band together, but there were only high school punks who kept tripping over their own peckers or old men with banjos. And where would we play anyway? There wasn't enough room in Skeeter's for a drum set. Screw it. Anyway, I was going to be a law man. Some plan.

I slowed up at the edge of Molly's yard, made sure the coast was clear. It wasn't a bad little house, three bedrooms, big front porch with a swing. About fifty years old but in good shape. Molly's room was on the side. I knocked on her window. Her step-dad drove a big rig and was out of town, but I didn't want to chance he'd come home early, so I always went to the window. Molly was two months shy of eighteen. Molly's mom had run off a year ago.

She came to the window, and I saw she hadn't been asleep. Sometimes she stayed up all night smoking cloves and reading books. She had a paperback of Ayn Rand in her hand. Big book. I generally didn't read anything thicker than *Road & Track*.

Molly looked good and weird which is what had attracted me to her in the first place. Dyed black hair like wet silk and black lipstick and a ring in her nose and white, white skin. She said when she turned eighteen she was out of this shit town and never looking back. I wasn't sure how I felt about that, but it was two months away. Sometimes two months is a long time. A lot can happen. Other times it's the blink of an eye.

"Come on," she whispered and opened the window all the way.

I scrambled through, and she shut the window again.

She started peeling off her clothes, but I stopped her. "No time. I just wanted to say hi. You want to go to the lake tomorrow?"

"What about Doris?"

"I'll tell her I pulled an extra shift or something. We can swim then lie out on the rocks."

"Too hot. I'll sunburn." And she kept taking off her clothes anyway. She had a silver ring through one raspberry nipple.

"Somebody killed Luke Jordan."

She was naked now, but the news stopped her from coming at me. "How?"

I shrugged, looked at her bright white skin and thought I could maybe do her quick and get back to the body before anyone missed me. "I think he came on to the wrong Mexican lady and somebody shot him." I sat on her bed, tugged down my sweatpants, erection springing into view. "They shot the shit out of him."

I tried to pull her on top of me, but she shrugged my arms away, knelt in front of me. I felt her hot breath down there. She stroked my sack, and then I felt wet, warm lips wrap around me. Her head started to bob, but slowly. My mouth fell open, a groan slipping out like a hiss. I felt it all up and down my body, like every nerve had been switched on.

Then she did climb on top, grunted as I entered her. "I applied to an art school in New York?"

"Oh yeah?" I thrust upward, finding a slow rhythm.

"I think I can get a scholarship. I have to, like, get all my stuff together into a portfolio and everything." She started to grind little circles, bit her lower lip. "You could come with me."

I couldn't do that, not with Doris and the boy. She knew that. Probably why she asked, so she could get credit for asking but with no danger I'd take her up on it. But it would be pretty cool to go to New York. I could probably get in with some band. I liked picturing myself there, but I hated thinking about a life I couldn't have.

She asked, "What's going to happen with Luke Jordan?"

"Don't know."

But I didn't want to talk anymore, and I thrust sort of desperate and quick, picking up speed, filling my hands with her ass, pulling her into me as I arched upward. I jerked and twitched, and we collapsed, pressed together in the heat and the sweat and the dark, dead night.

I lay there for a little while, time not seeming to mean much, but it was probably only like ten minutes. I got out of bed and pulled my sweatpants up. Molly turned over and pulled the sheet up to her chest. I waved bye and climbed out the window.

On the way back to Luke Jordan's truck, I tried to think if I felt bad about Molly or not. I told myself Doris would never know, so it wouldn't hurt her. And Molly would be gone in a couple months. Fuck, what did I know? Maybe I should just break it off now, but I probably couldn't do that any more than a junkie could give up the stuff. It's hard to do the right thing.

I made it back to the truck, stopped, blinked, circled the truck three times, a jittery sense of panic fluttering in my gut.

Luke Jordan wasn't there.

CHAPTER TWO

I ran around the truck looking for the body, looking up and down the street, my head spinning, trying to see everyplace at once. The world seemed to tilt a little and go wobbly.

Luke was gone.

"Oh . . . fuck."

There was this one time, a couple years ago, I was in Austin trying to catch a flight to Tulsa so I could come back for Mom's funeral. I was at the airport, and I felt for my wallet and it wasn't there. You know that feeling in your gut when something bad has happened and you know you can't fix it in time? Just like I knew I couldn't get home and back to the airport in time to make my flight. Take that bad gut feeling and multiply it by about two million and that's how I felt, on my hands and knees looking for Luke's corpse under his truck.

The difference is that the wallet turned up in another pocket. Luke Jordan didn't turn up.

I jogged up and down the streets, looking in every shadow. Maybe he hadn't been all the way dead, crawled off some place. A person thinks of shit like that, impossible miracle scenarios to somehow undo the calamity. I ended up back at the pickup truck, staring stupidly at the patch of road where his body should have been.

I was totally fucked.

Skeeter's was dark, but I went to the front window anyway, cupped my hands against the glass and looked inside. Maybe Wayne was still in there cleaning up. Maybe he'd seen something. Another miracle scenario, inventing it as I went along. Maybe Wayne came out and took the body inside. I knocked on the glass. No luck.

I lit a cigarette, tried to think what to do. I had completely and totally fucked this shit up. They don't put you on full time if you lose a body. More like I'd be fired, and then what? The boy went through a hundred diapers a day. There was no way we could make it on Doris's paycheck and tips. I'd have to get some shit road crew job or something. Hell. Doris was going to be pissed.

The three minute walk to the police station turned into ten as I meandered along waiting for an idea to fall out of the sky. I smoked a cigarette in front of the stationhouse door. Last one in the pack. I crumpled the pack, made like I was going to toss it into the street then remembered I was supposed to be the law. I held onto it. Not that I'd write myself a ticket for littering. But still.

It occurred to me maybe Billy was pulling some kind of prank on me, or maybe him and Karl together. Karl was one of the other deputies along with Amanda, but Amanda wouldn't fuck with me like that. Mom always said girls matured faster than boys, and some boys never got around to maturing at all. My first week on duty, Billy and Karl had radioed me all kinds of crazy shit, wild goose chasing me all over the county.

One time they called in that there were these high school girls skinny-dipping up to Red Hawk Pond. And that's a thirty mile drive. I couldn't get there fast enough to let them talk me out of arresting them. Sixty miles round trip. That's the sort of thing Karl thought was just hilarious.

I smiled, felt a little better. Sure that was it. The guys messing with me. Probably had Luke Jordan bagged up in the stationhouse right now, Billy and Karl laughing their asses off while I'm looking every which way for the body. Haze the new guy. No problem. Yeah, I was sure that was it. Jokers.

I stamped out the cigarette and went inside.

Billy looked up from his desk when I walked in, nodded at me. "Toby."

I flicked him a two-finger salute. I'd play it casual if that's how he wanted it. I tossed the empty cigarette pack in the trashcan.

Billy was scribbling at some papers, frowning. He didn't like paperwork. Who did?

I looked around the stationhouse. Not much to it. A couple of holding cells, a desk, gun cabinet, room in back. A ceiling fan turned so slow it was almost going backwards.

"You got any cigarettes?"

Billy shook his head without looking up. "You smoke too much."

I went into the back room. We each had a locker back there, mine at the end next to Amanda's. There was also a small safe and a filing cabinet. A door that led out back to the alley.

I opened my locker. My spare khaki deputy shirt hung on a hanger. I searched the pockets hoping for a pack of smokes but no luck. Damn. And the only place open was the Texaco up by the Interstate. Maybe I wanted smokes that bad, maybe not.

I heard something in the alley and opened the back door. This yellow dog I'd seen around was there again. Some kind of mix, Labrador hound mutt looking thing. Big. He'd knocked over this old metal trash can we kept back there and was pawing through everything.

"Git! Go on." I made a go-away motion.

The dog growled at me, and I backed into the station and shut the door. I went back to Billy at the desk.

"That dog's in the alley again."

"Yeah, I brought something for that." Billy opened the desk drawer and brought out this bright green gun, plastic. Shaped like some Buck Rogers laser ray gun.

"You want me to disintegrate him?" I asked.

"It's a squirt gun filled with ammonia," Billy said. "Trick I learned from a mailman. Stings the skin, especially around their nose and eyes. That'll send him packing."

"Okay." I took the squirt gun back out to the alley.

When I opened the door, the dog backed up a few steps, growled again, but mostly he just seemed scared. I kicked most of the trash back into the can with my foot, put the can back upright and stuck the lid on again. The dog wasn't growling at me any more. Just looking at me. He looked sad and hungry. I couldn't bring myself to zap him with the ammonia.

I opened the can, fished around until I found part of a hamburger, not too old. I put the lid back on the can, and set the green squirt gun on top. Then I squatted, held out the burger.

It took a few seconds, but he came forward and took the food. He let me scratch him behind the ears. Tail wagging. He appeared thin but not unhealthy. Probably make a good hunting dog for somebody. I watched him trot away down the alley.

I went back inside.

"You squirt him?" Billy asked.

"Sure." I sat on the edge of the desk.

Billy jerked upright. "Hey! Aren't you supposed to be standing over Luke Jordan?"

I smirked. "Like you don't know nothing about it."

He stood, leaned forward on the desk. "I'm not kidding, Toby. Who's out there with Jordan?"

Shit. Billy was serious. I had to rethink this. If he and Karl weren't messing with me than I really had just lost a fucking dead body. God damn, why does this shit happen to me?

"Look …" I tried to figure some way to say it that didn't sound like a colossal fuck up. "I just went to the bathroom for, like two minutes—"

"Cut to the chase," Billy said.

"I don't know where the body is."

"What?"

"I wasn't even gone two minutes."

"Oh, Christ, Toby!"

"I thought maybe you and Karl were fucking with me."

He rubbed his eyes and groaned.

"Fuck, I'm sorry." I reached for the radio. "Let me call the chief. I'll tell him."

"No," Billy said quickly. "Just give me a second."

He scratched his head, thinking. You could almost hear those rusty gears grinding.

"Look, maybe …" More chin scratching. "I think maybe I heard the chief say something to Karl about bagging the body. Not sure. Look, I'll check into it, okay?"

"I'd feel better if you called and asked him," I said. "I don't want to worry about it all night."

"I'll call him in a bit."

"It'll only take a minute or so and—"

"Go home, Toby."

I threw up my hands as I pushed off his desk and shuffled for the door. I could take a hint.

Outside I paused, stood in the shadow just to the side of the window. Billy was on the radio right after I left. Probably wanted to badmouth me to the chief when I couldn't hear. Shit. Well, fuck, I did lose a damn body. If they fired me, I'd have it coming. I'd screwed up big and didn't relish going home to tell Doris. Maybe I'd wait. Maybe things would be better in the morning, or at least I could figure some way to tell her that didn't make me look so stupid.

I jerked my head away from the stationhouse window when I heard the tires squeal. At the end of Main, I saw the nineteen-eighty-something Trans Am zig-zagging down the street. I recognized the car. I waited until they were close, stepped out of the shadows and held up a hand.

The Trans Am stood on its nose a bit stopping. I went over, leaned into the driver's side. Two teenage pukes. I'd seen them around but still couldn't come up with names. High school studs fucking around after dark. And on a school night. Was it my civic duty to hassle a couple of more or less harmless kids? Damn right.

"Out late, ain't you?"

The one in the passenger seat offered, "So what?"

The driver elbowed him. "Shut up, man."

Passenger Seat leaned down, got a peek at the star on my t-shirt. "Sorry." But he didn't seem too sorry. They're never really sorry.

"Should you be home?"

The driver shrugged, like some kind of half-assed apology. "We were going to the Texaco for Cokes."

"You got any cigarettes?"

They both patted their pockets, not sure which would be better, having cigarettes or not.

Little towns put out kids like this on an assembly line. Jeans and t-shirts and sneakers. One of them wore an Oklahoma State Cowboys cap, the orange so faded it looked like some vomit color. The driver had fuzz on his upper lip, probably told everyone it was a moustache. They played football and grab-ass until they graduated high school. Some would stick around and have dumb Okie babies, and others would go off to the big world and get the shit knocked out of them. I felt sorry for them, but I knew what they were thinking. They were looking at me and thinking when they got gone from this town, they'd *stay* gone.

I felt sorry for myself too because I hadn't.

The driver forked over a half-empty pack of Marlboro Lights. I took one, put it in my mouth. I thought about keeping the pack but gave it back. I didn't want to be that kind of cop.

"You best get on home. The chief catches you out late squealing tires, he won't be so nice about it."

That sobered them a little. The chief liked things nice and quiet and everybody knew it.

"We're sorry," said the driver. It sounded almost sincere this time.

"Don't be sorry. Just get on home."

"Okay."

They drove away.

I lit the Marlboro, smoked it. Stood there.

Shit.

I walked back down to Luke Jordan's pickup truck, locked it, closed the doors. I looked around again as if the body might have crawled back on its own. I still couldn't believe it. I climbed in the Chevy Nova and started driving south on State Road Six toward the Interstate.

The glow of the town lights faded after three minutes, and I was full into no-shit, outer space dark BFE Oklahoma. You could do that out here, just lose yourself in the perfect nothing of pitch black, except when you looked up. Stars big and glittering, not blotted out by city lights. Diamonds against black velvet and all that crap. Smart people had figured a thousand ways to say bright stars and dark night and have it sound like Shakespeare. But looking up, falling into the hugeness of it all, you could sort of see why the poets would take a stab at it.

I remember lying out by the lake at night with Doris, sharing a cheap bottle of wine, just looking up at the stars and enjoying feeling so small. I'd done the same thing with Molly too. Strange how it felt more like cheating than the actual screwing, sharing a moment like that.

I got the Nova up to about ninety. I flipped on the radio, passed through all the country stations until the dial landed on a Blind Melon song. I notched up the volume.

Usually nobody else on The Six this time of night. And so right then some headlights came up in the distance behind me. Gaining.

I just knew it was those fuckheads in the Trans Am. That's the problem with being a part time deputy with your star pinned on a ratty old Weezer t-shirt. Turn around five seconds later and these people are back at their shenanigans. Kids.

But when the car got closer, the headlights were all wrong. Not the Trans Am. It got maybe three car links behind me and slowed down to match speed. I slowed down too, thinking he might go around, but he hung in back there.

Ten more minutes to the Texaco at this rate, and I didn't want this joker on my ass the whole way, but it didn't look like he was going anywhere. I tapped the brakes, saw a wash of red taillights flare up in the rearview mirror. Take that, douche bag.

He backed off a fraction and stayed there. I was hoping to piss him off and make him go around. Okay, we'll try it the other way.

I stomped on the gas.

The V-8 roared, and I steadily pulled away. He couldn't keep up or wasn't trying. I saw the headlights shrink behind me as the speedometer needle edged toward ninety-five. The gas needle was going about as fast in the opposite direction. Fucking car drank unleaded like Doris went through Mountain Dew.

But she could run. A rusty shit-mobile on the outside, but I had my head under the hood every weekend making sure she purred like a damn pussycat. I was good about changing the oil and the filters. She could fly.

Only two pinpricks of light marked the sedan behind me. East dust, bozo.

I held it steady like that, only slowing a few minutes later when the fuzzy smear of light signaled the Interstate up ahead. There were no cars in the Texaco lot, but I wasn't worried about that since the place was open twenty-four hours. I parked up front and killed the engine.

A Coke and a pack of Winstons, and I'd be set. I checked for my wallet.

I didn't have it.

Hell. My wallet was in the back pocket of my blue jeans back at the trailer. I opened the glove compartment and started checking under the seats, gathering quarters and dimes. Not enough. I went for the nickels and pennies. Underneath my car seats: crumpled Winston packs, pens, ATM receipts, fast food wrappers. I was embarrassed. I liked keeping the Nova better than that.

There was enough for the Winstons but not the Coke. Priorities, baby, priorities.

I got out of the car and saw a car parked on the far side of the gas pumps that hadn't been there ten seconds ago. If it had been the car tailing me down The Six, it sure as hell could have caught up with me if it had wanted to. A totally cherry Ford Mustang Mach 1. And it was tricked out too. That car could chew up my Nova and shit it out the tailpipe no problem. Maybe it wasn't them.

I went inside for the cigarettes.

There was a new girl on the counter.

"Where's Wally?"

"I don't know no Wally." Hick accent so thick you'd need a hacksaw to get through it. She flipped through an issue of *Modern Bride.* Not so bad looking. Buck teeth. Freckles.

"Larson hire you?"

She nodded. "Started last night." She put her face back into the *Modern Bride.*

"You getting married?"

"No."

"Pack of Winstons." I plunked the change on the counter in a messy pile.

She scraped it up and dumped it into the register without counting.

I opened the pack, stuck one in my mouth.

"You can't smoke in here."

I tapped my thumb against the star on my shirt. "It's okay. I give myself permission."

"You send away for that? My nine-year-old nephew got one in a kid's meal."

I let that go and ambled past the front window. The Mach 1 was still sitting out there. I tried to see in the front window without looking like I was looking, but I couldn't see anyone. He wasn't pumping gas or anything. I suppose I could have gone over there and stuck my head in the window like I did with the kids in the Trans Am, but I didn't. I don't know why. I just didn't.

"You ever see that car before?"

"Nope."

I circled the store once like I was still shopping. The car still sat out there. I didn't want to go outside.

"Well, I guess I'd better get a move on. You have a good night."

The freckled girl waved without looking up. She was back at her magazine.

I went outside, kept the Ford in my peripheral vision all the way back to the Nova. I half expected it to crank up with fire in the headlights like devil eyes. I forced myself to move slow, put on the seatbelt, stick the key into the ignition. The hell if I was going to spook myself with crap about a devil car. My imagination was fucking with me.

I sat in my car with the window rolled down, my back slick with sweat. I watched the freckled girl through the store window. She flipped pages in the magazine. Why did women read stuff like that? She didn't live in Coyote Crossing or I'd have seen her. I glanced over at the Mustang, and it just sat there being a Mustang. I sucked on my cigarette, leaned my head out the window and blew smoke at the moon. Big green cheese. Banana cream pie in the sky. The man in the moon had bad skin. The Mustang just sat there. I started the Nova and drove back north on The Six.

Back in the thick Okie night. I put the Nova in the center of the road and let it eat up the lines like Pac Man. Last Christmas Doris got this computer game that hooked to the TV, a bunch of vintage video games like Pac Man and Galaga. By vintage I guess they meant old crappy games you could get cheap. We stayed up late and played it some nights when we finally got the boy to sleep. When I got on full time with the department, I was going to get one of those new Wii games Nintendo makes.

I was humming along fine, sucking on a fresh Winston. Maybe three minutes and I saw the headlights in my rearview mirror again.

And this time they did look like the devil's eyes.

CHAPTER THREE

Truth was I had a vivid imagination. My mother always said so. Too vivid. I hated the barn at night, back when the family had a few acres south of here. Up until I was twelve years old, I hated to go out there. The tools and the tractor and hay would make strange shapes in the shadows. A kid can imagine any kind of monster in the dark. Any sort of shape under the moonlight. A scurrying barn rat can sound like anything.

And Halloween night after a few scary movies? Forget it. You couldn't have paid me a thousand dollars to go out to the barn. I remembered this one movie about killer spiders that bred in a barn, all full of webs and everything. Just forget it.

Dad lost that barn to back taxes then died. Two sure things in as many months.

But I had that crazy imagination.

It was pretty easy for me to imagine undead Luke Jordan behind the wheel of the devil Mustang behind me. There was never any traffic this time of night on The Six. Getting followed all the way to the Texaco *and* back? No way.

Okay, so probably it wasn't the undead. But who?

I drove faster.

The car got up to about a hundred yards behind me and stayed there. Coyote Crossing loomed in the distance, and I stepped on the gas, slowed down again as I pulled into town but with a little more space between me and my tail. I took the first left without slowing or signaling, then another quick right into the alley behind the firehouse before the guy behind me could see where I was going. I backed up behind a dumpster and killed the headlights. If I leaned forward over the steering wheel, I could just see the road around the edge of the dumpster.

At first, nothing happened, and I thought I'd made a mistake. Then a wash of yellow light crept along the road, followed by the Mach 1. It cruised along about fifteen miles per hour, maybe looking for me, maybe not. It kept going. I sat there and smoked a cigarette. When the Mustang didn't come back, I put the Nova in gear and eased out of the alley.

■ ■ ■ ■

I drove back down Main Street, heading toward the trailer park west of town. I kept glancing in the rearview mirror, but the headlights didn't come back. I blew out a relieved gust of breath.

The town fizzled out again heading west, and I was back into raw wilderness, but not for so long this time. Two minutes later I hit the area near my home, a sorry little hamburger joint called Sam's, a gas station, and an out-of-business used car lot. Once or twice a month, some folks used the old car lot to set up a flea market. Two hundred yards later, I turned into the park entrance, a dingy collection of twenty trailers all waiting for a twister to come along and put them out of their misery.

I pulled in next to Doris's old, yellow Monte Carlo. I let the Nova run, flipped around the radio dial until I heard a Garbage song and left it. Lit another cigarette. I didn't know if I wanted Doris to be awake or not. I felt like talking, didn't feel like being alone. When you're with somebody who's asleep, you're basically alone. Unless they're curled up against you maybe. That's different.

When I came back to Coyote Crossing for Mom's funeral, I was told I had inherited the trailer. It was nothing fancy or nice, but it was more than I'd had before. It was a place to flop while I got my plan together. Maybe I'd sell it and go to California or New Orleans or, hell, even London. You could hook up with all kinds of funky bands in London. Anyway that's what I thought, weep my last tears over Mom's grave then light out free as a bird on the big adventure of my life.

The night after the funeral a couple of old high school pals took me out to cheer me up with some beer and somebody's cousin's friend was there and felt so sorry for me that she took me out to her cousin's Buick and hopped right on top of me and eased the pain of my loss, in that grunting, hunched-up way that makes us forget all about death. Twice. That was Doris. We saw each other a few more times. She seemed impressed I had my own trailer, said I was lucky to live on my own because she had to live with her folks. I told her she was lucky to still have folks, and I think that embarrassed her. She always just said things. But I was only hanging around town long enough to sell the trailer anyway.

Then one day Doris up and tells me she's pregnant. Then her father's right there on the front porch asking me if I'm going to do the right thing. Then I'm married. Then I'm a daddy. It happened so fast, it was like it was happening to somebody esle. Life can run you over like that when it comes at you so much at one time.

Which brings me to now, sitting in the Nova, wondering if I wanted Doris to be awake or not. Some nights yes, others no.

I finished the cigarette and went inside as quietly as I could. I didn't want to wake the boy. That's the first thing you learn as a parent. When they finally get to sleep, you do anything to keep them that way.

Every step I took creaked and rocked the trailer. Swear to God, a good sneeze would explode the place. I kicked off my shoes, tip-toed into the bathroom, looked in the mirror.

I looked like hell. Dark under the eyes. The stubble was getting a little out of hand, but I winced at the thought of shaving. Doris used my disposables to shave her legs. Might as well scrape my face with a spatula. I needed a haircut. It was in that in-between stage where it wasn't short enough to look tidy, but not long enough to look cool. I felt greasy, and my mouth tasted like too many cigarettes.

Everybody said I smoked too much. They were right.

I stripped, reached in the shower and turned the water lukewarm.

■ ■ ■ ■

I stepped in and soaped up, closed my eyes and let the spray hit my face. Some of the tension drained out of my shoulders, and I stood there until the water went cold. The trailer's hot water heater might as well have been the size of a thermos. I dried off with an almost clean towel.

I got lucky with a fresh laundry basket on the toilet and slipped into a pair of clean boxers. A shower and clean underwear can make anyone feel human again.

I went to the boy's room and looked inside. He made a fat little lump under his blue blanket, and I heard his steady breathing. He looked perfect. There were those crazy times, when the boy was screaming, a loaded diaper, the trailer a mess, Doris calling to say she'd be late, and I thought how could I do it anymore? How was it possible? All I had to do was look at the boy asleep and it was all good again. He was starting to walk and say words. I went to our bedroom, closed the door behind me and slipped in next to Doris.

She smelled nice, like Pantene. Not like fried eggs and bacon grease when she first gets in from work. Doris had a nice round shape in the hips, full breasts. It would probably all droop and go to fat in a few years like her mother, but right now it was still pretty good. She had a broad tan back, and she slept naked, so I moved in behind her and spooned. I put my nose in her blond hair and stayed like that a minute. I knew she was awake because she backed her ass into my crotch, grinding back at me a little until I took the hint. I reached around and cupped a breast and felt her hand slip back and into my boxers, guiding me into her. She gasped very softly as the tip went in, sort of cooed as the rest slid home. I settled into a rhythm, kissing the back of her neck.

Sex with Doris was always familiar and comfortable. Not like the reckless thunderstorm of passion with Molly. With Molly I felt my teeth rattle, muscles strained. Both of us went at it like we were trying to win something. Doris was like easing into a warm bath. I liked having both.

I felt Doris go rigid next to me and swallow a moan. She was never loud. I sped up my hip thrusts to keep pace and came thirty seconds later. Her being on the pill made spontaneous humps more possible. It was so convenient, I'd told Molly to get on the pill too.

As soon as I'd shuddered to a stop, Doris rolled out of bed, and I could hear her in the bathroom.

Maybe I dozed some after that, but I wasn't sure. Couldn't have been more than five minutes. The trailer's air conditioning hummed full blast to keep it bearable. I lay there in the darkness with my eyes open, thinking the same old thoughts. What to tell Doris when I got fired. What to do when Molly left. How to feed the boy and keep him in diapers and pay the doctor when he got sick. I could think these thoughts in a circle so fast it made my stomach ache, but I never came up with any answers.

I sat up in bed, swung my feet over the side. God, I just wanted to go to sleep. Hell.

I got up, paused in the hall to peek through the blinds. I half expected to see a Mach 1 cruising the trailer park then felt stupid. Some guy out for a drive and I get all

jumpy. I wondered if the chief had heard about my stupidity yet. I thought about calling Billy at the stationhouse
but went into the boy's room instead.

Toby Austin Sawyer Jr. was perfect and pink. He'd
kicked the blue blanket off one leg, and I saw Doris had
put him in the Bob the Builder pajamas. He was the best
looking boy in the world.

■　■　■　■

At that moment the need to scoop him out of the crib and
hold him firm against my chest nearly overcame me. Even
if it woke him up. He was such a heavy little ham hock.
Thick. He'd probably be a linebacker. Get a football scholarship to Harvard and be a brain surgeon. My boy.

I didn't pick him up. I satisfied myself with stroking his
forehead. He stirred, and I jerked my hand back, but he did-
n't wake. Doris would be turbo pissed off if I woke him up.

I pulled the rocking chair close to the crib and sat
awhile looking at him. A little night light shaped like a blue
fishbowl cast a soft glow on everything, all the second-hand
toys and stuffed animals. Even the crib and rocking chair
had come from Doris's older sister. My folks were dead,
but Doris's mom and dad did a pretty good job bringing
toys and clothes. We had enough. It was close, but we were
just making it. Of course, that was probably about to
change.

Toby Junior. TJ. I got this tight, anxious feeling whenever I looked at him and thought something could go wrong or he'd get sick or any little thing might not be right somehow. Like iron fingers grabbing my chest and squeezing. I folded my arms over the edge of the crib and put my head down, sat there a while.

The boy's gentle breathing was like some kind of lullaby.

CHAPTER FOUR

Our cramped living room led right into the cramped kitchen, so Doris could stand at the counter making coffee and still see the television. She had a rerun of *The Real World* on with the sound down almost to nothing. Some dude was yelling at the *Real World* kids because they were all supposed to be up early for some project thing, but they slept in instead. What the hell was the big deal?

I said, "You're staying up?"

She shrugged, watching the coffee drip. "I can't go back to sleep now."

"I'll take a cup of that."

"When it's finished."

"Pour me a cup now," I told her.

"It's only halfway through. It won't taste right."

"I don't mind."

"*I* mind." She *tsked*, shook her head. "Damn it, who's making this fucking coffee?"

"There's a cut off if you take the pot out before it's finished. So it doesn't spill." I put that obnoxious patient sound in my voice, like I was talking to a little kid. "The coffee maker is designed specifically so you can do that."

"We've had this conversation already."

And there you pretty much had the whole marriage. We fit together good in bed, worked together nice, folding laundry together or doing the dishes, her washing and me drying and putting them back in the cabinet. My mom had been big on companionable silence. Needless talk only causes trouble, she'd told me once. Maybe she was right because Doris and I sure got into it whenever one of us opened our yaps. Something was always eating one of us.

I decided I'd better say something nice. "You don't look so fat."

She frowned. "What?"

"Your ass, I mean."

"Fuck you, Toby."

"Shit, that's not how I meant it, okay?" She stood there in plain white panties and my Green Day t-shirt, and I thought she looked fine. "You were looking in the mirror the other day, remember? And you said you thought it was getting big. I'm just saying I think it's fine."

"Whatever. You want this coffee now?"

"Okay."

She poured two cups and brought them to the couch. She didn't sit close to me but not so far away either. She handed me a plain white cup of black coffee. Her mug was bigger and with a sunset clouds scene and some scripture on the side. John 3:16, I think.

I sipped. She sipped. We watched *The Real World* with the sound down.

I tried some more conversation like this: "When do you go into work?"

"You know what time. Seven like always."

Then I tried this: "How's your sister?"

"You don't even like her."

I sipped coffee and shut up.

Real World ended and *Super Sweet Sixteen* came on. Little girls having fancy birthday parties. This show made me pissed off and depressed at the same time. That these spoiled kids could have it so good and it still wasn't enough. This one girl got a brand new BMW for her sixteenth birthday but pissed and moaned it was the wrong color. Jesus. Slap that bitch.

"Oh, cool," Doris said. "I wish I'd had a big party like that when I was sixteen."

We watched a few minutes.

Finally she asked, "What was the problem?"

I looked at her. "With what?"

"What do you think? Taking off at midnight with your pistol, that's what. What did the chief want?"

"Oh." I sipped coffee. "Somebody killed Luke Jordan."

I saw the blood drain from her face. Like somebody pulled a plug and it all leaked right out, her eyes round with startled confusion. I wasn't sure what surprised me more. Her reaction or that fact she was trying to hide it.

"Dead?"

"Yeah."

"Why did—" She paused, cleared her throat. "How?"

"Wayne said he was making a play for some Mexican chick in Skeeter's. Jealous boyfriend maybe. Shot the crap out of him." I didn't tell her the rest of it, losing the body and all. I didn't have the heart for that conversation, maybe never would.

Maybe I could get a job at the fertilizer plant. That was an hour drive each way, but I'd be full time with benefits too. Maybe I could go over there and get the job and then even tell Doris I quit the department on purpose to bring in more money. She'd be glad about that. Hell, it might even work. And if I made enough she could quit the waitress job and take care of the boy full time.

"Maybe it was some kind of mistake," she said.

I blinked. "What?'

"Maybe he was just talking to that Mexican girl, and it was some kind of misunderstanding."

I shrugged, didn't see what difference that made. "Luke Jordan's just as dead either way."

She got up and went into the kitchen. I thought about asking her for more coffee but didn't. The Super Sweet Sixteen girl was pissing and moaning because her daddy got the wrong boy band to play at her party. It should be legal just to punch these people. No jail time. Case dismissed.

Doris came back, stood at the end of the couch.

"Toby?"

"Yeah?"

"Let's go to Houston. My sister will put us up until we get work. I can waitress anywhere. We have to try something different."

That was my chance right then. I could tell her okay, let's sell the trailer for moving money and go to Houston and remake our lives from the ground up. I was going to get shit-canned anyway. I had no prospects. Even my idea about the fertilizer plant seemed pretty feeble now. Molly would be gone soon. No reason in the world not to give Doris's idea serious consideration.

But for some reason I said, "I don't know. Doesn't sound like a good idea."

"You never liked my sister."

"This again."

She balled up one of her little fists and hit me in the arm. It didn't hurt. Much. She went back into the kitchen.

I could feel her fuming in there. You could almost see the anger radiating around her, like heat waves off hot asphalt.

"Don't be like that."

"You're stupid." Her voice sounded funny, kind of shaky.

"I don't need this."

"Fuck you." Plenty of venom. Doris never did need much of an excuse to start some shit, but this was sudden even for her.

"What's eating you?"

"I'm, like, all trying to better our life and stuff, and you're just not even being cool about it. You never listen to me."

Bullshit. All I ever did was listen to her run her mouth, complaining about anything and everything. She'd get home from work and start right in and wouldn't shut it until she fell asleep or I left for work. She was like some kind of Energizer Bunny nonstop bitch machine. Or she'd drop the boy in the playpen with a few toys and sit in front of the TV for hours and hours. Or on the phone with her sister for a million hours at a time. She needed three more husbands, so we could all take shifts listening to her.

"We'll talk about it later. Just keep it down for now, okay? You'll wake the boy."

"The boy!" She scoffed. "You don't have that brat hanging on you every damn minute when you get home from work. I'm *tired*, Toby. I'm tired of everything. Tired of this shit town."

Tired of this shit town. Everyone sang the same song. Molly. Doris. Every other stud fresh out of high school with more balls than brains, off to conquer the world. They didn't know what it was like out there. None of them did.

I pushed myself off the couch, went to the bathroom and took the tin star off my dirty Weezer shirt. It wasn't really tin, I guess. That's just something the chief said when he gave it to me. *Here's your tin star, Deputy.* Back in my bedroom, I went into the closet, came out with a clean khaki uniform shirt, patch on the sleeve. I pinned the star over the right pocket. I put on a clean pair of jeans. Sweat socks and hiking boots.

I went back into the kitchen. Doris stood with her hands on the counter facing away from me. I took down one of the travel mugs with a lid, filled it with coffee and snugged the lid on.

"I'm going back out. Forgot to do a few things at the station." And I couldn't stay around when she was like this. Anywhere was better than here.

She didn't say anything.

I went back in our bedroom, grabbed the straw cowboy hat off the dresser and wore it back on my head. Now I looked like the law.

Doris still leaned on the counter when I went back in the kitchen. By now she was usually yelling something at me. I didn't know if I should be grateful or not. I put a hand on her shoulder to turn her around, and she let me.

Her eyes were wet and red, face snotty from crying.

"I want to go to my sister's." She said it like she hardly had any breath left. Like she might fall down any minute.

"I promise we'll talk about it when you get off work. We'll make some kind of plan."

She didn't say anything. Maybe she didn't believe me.

I headed for the door. She worried me. "I'll be back before you go to work."

I left, closed the trailer door quietly, so I didn't wake the boy. After I got into the Nova, I remembered I didn't have my gun. Then I remembered it was under the seat. I fished it out and put it on the passenger seat. Hell, I hadn't even locked the car door. I'd have to be more careful. I needed to pay more attention to things. And when the boy got older too. Can't leave a gun around where a kid can find it.

The kitchen light didn't go out, and I knew Doris was still up. The TV lights flickered. Maybe I should go back in there. I hated leaving her so upset, but what could I do? I couldn't fix anything. Maybe that's why she was crying. Maybe if we could just earn a little more money somehow. Maybe if I was a better man.

Maybe if I'd been a better musician. Maybe a lot of things.

I remembered when the band broke up. The lead singer's dad got tired of his son screwing off. That's what he called our band. Screwing off, like we weren't serious about our music. Jerk. But he told his son he'd pay for college and there went our singer. The drummer joined the Army, and the bass player met some girl. A new course at the local police academy was about to start, and the idea of me with a gun on my hip and mirrored sunglasses suddenly seemed pretty sweet. Fourteen weeks of pushups and regulations. I graduated at the bottom of my class, but there I was ready to clean up some city like fucking Serpico, baby. All that stuff I learned about codes and violations flew out of my head an hour later. Pretty much how I got through high school.

Six days later I got the letter about Mom.

Hell.

I put the Nova in reverse and backed out. I drove out of the trailer park, back toward town. Maybe I could find the chief, apologize for my screw-up. He liked me. He wouldn't protect me too far if I screwed up bad enough. He was a by-the-book man, and I'd have to take my lumps. But maybe we could work something out.

Thirty seconds later the headlights were back in the rearview mirror.

Perfect.

CHAPTER FIVE

Now I was getting pissed off.

No way this was a coincidence. Somebody was fucking with me.

I kept it at the speed limit all the way into town, the car on my tail about two hundred yards back. I couldn't tell if it was the same car as before, but my gut told me it was. I drove along Main Street and parked in front of the station. As I got out of the car, I saw the Mustang turn right a block back.

I tried the stationhouse door. Locked. The lights were on, so I knocked, but nobody answered. I found the right key on my ring, unlocked the door and went inside. I called for Billy but didn't get a reply. I thought about calling him or the chief on the radio but figured that might piss them off since I was supposed to be home. A car passed outside, headlights seeping through the blinds. I waited a minute but the headlights didn't come back.

I went out the back door and into the alley, shut and locked the door behind me. I wondered if that dog was still around. Probably off someplace sleeping peacefully. Smart dog. I walked down the alley behind the hardware store and the fire house, all the windows dark. I cut up the next street and crossed Main after looking both ways to make sure it was deserted. I walked the couple blocks to Molly's.

This time her stepdad's Peterbilt sat in front of the house. Not the trailer, just the cab. He must've delivered his load ahead of schedule and come home. I hesitated under the big scrub oak in her front yard and wondered if it was safe to knock on her window. If her old man followed his routine he'd either be blitzed on Jim Beam in front of the TV or sleeping it off by now. Probably he was ragged out from a long haul, so I was guessing bed. I crept up to Molly's dark window and knocked.

I gave her twenty seconds and knocked again. I almost gave up when she came to the window and lifted it open.

"Go on, Toby. Roy's back."

Roy. Didn't that just sound like a drunken redneck stepfather name?

"He's asleep, ain't he?"

She glanced over her shoulder back into the dark of her room, thought about it. "Okay, but just for a little bit."

She stepped back from the window, and I crawled in.

The clove smell had faded some. The room was air-conditioner cold and felt nice after being outside, but I could see gooseflesh on Molly's arms in the light of the streetlamp, her nipples straining against the fabric of her black tank top. She wore that and white cotton panties. Her hair was a little mashed on one side, so she'd probably been sleeping a while.

"I'm getting back under the covers." She crawled into bed.

I stayed at her window, wondering if the Mustang would come down her street any moment, but I didn't see anything.

"What do you want, Toby? I don't want to fuck anymore." Her voice drifted from a vague lump under the comforter. Her fat stepdad liked to crank the air down arctic style.

"I just need to hide out a minute." I hesitated. "I think I'm in deep shit, Molly."

"Why?"

"Remember, I told you Luke Jordan was dead?"

A pause. "You killed him?"

"No! Hell. Come on."

"What then?"

"I lost the body."

She laughed.

"It's not very Goddamn funny."

"Yes it is."

"There are some guys after me, I think. They keep following me."

She stopped laughing. "Maybe it's Luke's brothers."

"What for?"

"Well, if you ... Toby, if you killed Luke Jordan, I wouldn't tell anyone."

"Why the hell would I kill Luke, for fuck's sake?"

Her voice got real small. "No reason."

"Anyway it's some car I've never seen in town before. Big-ass, tricked out Ford Mustang. Mach 1 with a V-8 like a fucking rocket engine."

"Somebody from out of town."

"Yeah."

And that didn't help me a damn bit. Why would somebody randomly breeze into town and take a sudden interest in freaking me out? The answer: it wasn't random, I was just too thick to know why. Okay, if I wanted to be a deputy so bad, then it was time to start thinking like one. Think smart. Okay, dipshit, what's the only other thing of interest that's happened? A dead Luke Jordan. So what's the connection? You don't know, do you, you dumb motherfucker?

Hell.

"You went quiet," Molly whispered. "You okay?"

"I'm thinking."

"Solve anything?"

"Thinking's not my main strength."

"Come get in bed."

I went to the bed, stood at the edge. If I got in, I'd have a hell of a time getting out again. I wanted sleep. I wanted to stretch out next to Molly, pull that comforter over our heads and forget about everything else. But I wasn't supposed to sleep here, and I for damn sure wasn't supposed to wake up here.

She sat up, took my hand. "Come on."

I shook my head. "Can't do it. Oh, man, I want to, but I can't."

She let go of my hand, her fingers dragging across my crotch. I felt the spark of electricity, things stirring to life. "I bet I can change your mind."

"Really, Molly. I'd better go. I have to find out what's going on."

Her hands worked my zipper, reached in and fished me out. I was semi-erect. She started fondling. It took a minute or so, but I managed another erection, found myself thrusting against her fist. I didn't think there was anything left after the night I'd had, but the thought of getting inside Molly again made me dizzy. Her head leaned in, and I felt her hot breath as her mouth edged closer.

The banging fists on her bedroom door sent my heart into my throat. "Open this Goddamn door!" Roy.

Molly shoved me away. "The closet!" Her whisper was a frightened hiss.

I scooted to her closet, my erection wagging and deflating but not fast enough. I closed the door, saw the light leak underneath. Molly had gotten up, switched on the light, probably slipping into her robe. The banging on the door increased.

"Okay!" she yelled. "Two seconds."

I heard the door creak open, the heavy slouch of Roy pushing his way in.

"What the fuck's going on in here?" A booze slur in Roy's voice.

"What do you mean?"

"You talking to somebody?"

"I was on the phone."

"Who with?"

I lost track of the interrogation, realized my pecker was still dangling out of my fly. I reached to zip it up fast, caught the tip in the zipper.

I bit my lip to keep back a yelp, tears quickly filling my eyes. Oh, fucking shit! Felt like a hot match head on the end of my dick. I tried to work the zipper down slowly, sweat bubbling on my forehead and behind my ears. The argument between Molly and Roy was getting louder, but I tuned it out, still trying to work my zipper without ripping a hole in my dick.

There was a smear of warm blood on my fingers when I finally unjammed the skin from the zipper. I wanted to weep, but the blinding hot pain slowly subsided. I had to stop myself from moaning relief.

I heard "Goddamn little cunt" and the smack of skin on skin so loud it made me jump. Sounds of a struggle, grunting. I put my hand on the closet doorknob, hesitated, not quite ready to explain what I was doing in this underage girl's closet. It was difficult to just stand there and listen, but I made myself be patient.

Then I heard Molly scream, "Leave me the fuck alone!" and storm out of the room.

Roy chased after her with, "Don't turn your back on me!"

I waited another moment, heard the muffled argument elsewhere in the house. I pushed the door open and headed for the window when I saw the coast was clear, bumped my shin on the way out. I tumbled down, sprawled in a pile on her yard.

"Shit."

I stood slowly, still a vague sting at the tip of my dick, my right shin throbbing.

I looked at the house, telling my body to turn around and go about the business of the night, but I knew I couldn't do that. Molly had told me she'd caught her stepdad looking at her a bunch of times, and not a good kind of look. Sort of creepy and licking his lips, so Molly locked her door every night before bed. If I walked away, and anything happened to her, it would be my fault.

I went up the front steps, knocked, waited, knocked some more.

The porch light came on, and I heard the rattle of chains and locks and then the door opened. Roy stood swaying, looking at me with one eye closed. A cloud of bourbon almost knocked me back down the steps.

"What do you want?"

"Neighbors called in a domestic dispute. I need to know the trouble."

"Shit." Roy snorted. "I know you. I know why you're here."

"Been drinking tonight, sir?"

"Fuck you."

"Roy, maybe you'd better spend the night with a friend so there's no problem here after I leave. Grab somebody's couch and sleep it off."

Another snort. "You think I take that star on your chest seriously? You think anybody does?"

"This is serious police business, Roy."

"Kiss my ass." He started to close the door.

I shoved my leg in, pushed the door open again. "Hold on."

"Get your fucking hands off—"

He came at me, a sloppy leap, and I stepped aside. He stumbled down the porch steps, tried to turn and punch at me while he was falling and he ended up on his ass at the bottom. He winced, rubbed a bruised elbow.

"Settle down, Roy."

"You little—you fucking—prick." He heaved out the words between breaths, wheezing and red faced, made a grab at my pants.

I put a boot against his shoulder and kicked him back. He sprawled, looked straight up in the sky, still muttering curses. I didn't feel like a hero picking on a drunk fat man twice my age, but I wasn't broken up about it either. I wasn't looking to defend Molly's honor with some kind of a fair fight, and if Roy was too blitzed to hit back that was all right by me. Frankly, it felt good to dominate the situation for a change.

"You want me to call Chief Krueger? Maybe you'll listen to him."

Roy sighed out a groan.

"Maybe you'd take the chief more seriously. What do you say about that, Roy?"

He didn't say anything.

"How about it? Get the chief on the horn?"

"Okay, I fucking get it," Roy said. "I'll go to Howard Boyle's house. It's only two blocks."

"Hand over your keys."

"Oh, now what the fuck for? Jesus."

"I can't have you sneaking back five minutes after I'm gone," I told him. "You can pick up the keys at the station house in the morning."

He fished the keys out of his pocket and tossed them to me.

I turned back to the house, the open front door. "Molly, you lock up after we leave."

"Okay." Her voice floated closer than expected from the dark innards of the house. I supposed she'd been listening the whole time.

"Come on, Roy. I'll walk you." I offered my hand.

He took it, and I pulled him up. He dusted himself off with clumsy ham hands. All the fight had gone out of him, and I think if I'd told him to lie down right there on the lawn and go to sleep he'd have done it. All I wanted was for him to get to sleep somewhere.

We walked in and out of dim blotches of street light on the way to Howard Boyle's house. Roy smelled like booze and sweat. He put one foot in front of the other like he couldn't believe he was alive, like sooner or later gravity would just say *that's enough of you* and drag him right down.

"Her mother takes off, and I'm left to do everything. I mean, what the hell. I married her and she had a kid and all. I took her in. Both of them. Then Molly's mother just fucking takes off. And now I got this girl on my hands like some kind of alien, the way she dresses and that freaky, dark-ass music she listens to."

I already knew Roy's story, but he told it so sad I almost felt sorry for him.

Almost.

"She's going to be out of your hair soon," I said. "You know once she's off to college she'll never come back. Not here." Saying it out loud like that hit me right in the gut. "Anyway, you can behave yourself until then."

"Can't be soon enough," Roy said. "Get my friggin' life back."

Some life.

Howard Boyle's house was at the end of the street where the neighborhood petered out and blended into open field, and a half-wrecked windmill beyond. There were a hundred places like this in Oklahoma where a town suddenly stopped and you stood staring into wide open nothing. Boyle's house wasn't much more than a shabby shotgun shack, but it still had more room than my trailer. We climbed the steps, knocked on the door. It took a long time for Howard to flip on the porch light and open up.

Howard ran the tire and lube store in town. He'd inherited it from his daddy and hit the skids in the late eighties. Some rich guy from Tulsa who made a habit of snatching up troubled businesses for a song bought the place but kept Howard on to run it. Looking at the slackbellied, balding fifty-something wreck in front of me, I saw a man who didn't have a damn thing to look forward to when he got up each morning. No family. No legacy. No talent for anything accept changing a tire. Even his boxer shorts looked like they weren't hiding much. Probably the perfect drinking buddy for old Roy. Sure.

Howard squinted at us and scratched his belly. "What time is it?"

"Late," I said. "Or early. Depends if you're coming or going."

"You arrest Roy?"

"Not tonight. We thought he might crash on your couch."

Howard made a face, like maybe he wanted to know why but was just too tired to ask. "Yeah, okay."

Roy started into the house, paused in the doorway. "What's a man supposed to do? I mean for fuck's sake, can you tell me that? How does a man know?"

I really couldn't say what he was getting at, but I said, "We just do our best as we go along, I guess. And maybe it'll seem like the right thing when we look back on it later."

This seemed to satisfy him. He nodded and went inside. Howard followed him in and turned off the porch light.

I lit a cigarette and smoked my way back the way we'd come. *What's a man supposed to do? How does a man know?* Damn right. Preach it, Roy. From the mouth of babes, the

Good Book said. But once in a while a tumble-down drunk got it right too. Roy didn't have the answers any more that I did, but at least he knew the questions. And that's half the battle.

I smoked and walked and wondered if that was all bullshit or not.

When I got back to Main Street, I saw the Ford Mustang Mach 1 parked right behind my Nova.

CHAPTER SIX

I was halfway across the street, and they didn't see me at first, the three Mexicans standing around the Nova looking through the windows. I froze, puffed the cigarette, and wondered what to do.

I didn't do anything. They saw me first.

They nudged each other, pointed in my direction, stood up straight and moved away from the Nova. I could either haul ass or square my shoulders and get all Johnny Law.

"What seems to be the trouble here, gentleman?" I said.

I'm just not very smart.

They edged closer, taking it slow, looking me over.

All three wore silk shirts, buttons undone to reveal gold jewelry. The one in the lead wore a black shirt. His head was shaved, gold hoop earrings. The two behind him were in red, beards, various tattoos. It looked like somebody had driven though town and puked a Los Lobos tribute band into the street.

One of the redshirts fired off some syllables in Spanish, and I caught the word *pistola*.

The one in the black shirt looked me over again and shook his head. "No."

My hand automatically went to my belt. No gun. Shit. It was still in the Nova.

The Mexicans grinned and came at me.

I plucked the Winston out of my mouth and flicked it at the lead guy's face. It bounced off his cheek, orange sparks flying, not really doing any damage, but he flinched and pulled up short. I went low and jabbed a fist in his ribs, heard some of the air go out of him. A second quick punch for good measure.

Some personal history: When you've played guitar in as many roadside honky-tonk shitholes as I have, you learn to throw a few punches. You learn that hesitation can earn you a black eye and a fat lip.

The two red shirts closed in on either side. I felt the stars go off hot behind my eyes as a fist slammed into my face.

Some additional personal history: I always took more than I dished out.

They grabbed at me fast, trying to wrestle me down. I kicked out, connected my heel with something and heard a grunt. More fists in my gut and a blow to the back of my head, and I oozed down to the asphalt.

I lay there a second with the vague sense of them standing over me. Pressure on my chest. My eyes focused and I saw it was a boot, the bald one keeping me down with a foot on the chest. The other two went through my pockets.

I found my voice and managed, "What the hell, man?"

"*Quiate tu boca.*"

Right.

One of the red shirts yanked a set of keys out of my pocket, held them up and jingled them. "*Aqui.*"

They chattered at each other some more, and I got the idea they were talking about what to do with me. I thought about shoving the guy's boot off my chest and making a run for it, but I still had cartoon tweety-birds circling my head, and I was hoping I could think of some better plan that didn't involve me running and having three Mexicans jump on my back.

I got lucky. Headlights sparked into view at the end of Main, coming right toward our little scene in the street. The Mexicans jabbered at each other again, and one of the red shirts gave me a goodbye kick in the ribs before they all jumped back in their muscle car. They squealed the tires as they tore away from the curb. I flinched away as a tire came within three inches of my head.

I sat up, watched the taillights vanish the other direction out of town. I wasn't exactly sure what had happened. The other car came up behind me, and I twisted to look, muscles sore, a vague pain through my whole body.

The kid stuck his head out of the window of the Trans Am. "You okay, man?"

I stood slowly, a miserable groan leaking out of me. "I told you to go home." His mouthy pal wasn't in the passenger seat anymore.

"Who was that just drove off?" he asked.

"Bad guys."

"You going to chase them?"

"Can't. They got my keys." I patted my pockets, was surprised to feel a lump and pulled out my set of keys. "Wait." I looked at them. Yep. They were mine. I snapped my fingers. The Mexicans had grabbed Roy's keys. Ha. Take that, fucking beaners.

"I'm serious this time," I told the Trans Am kid. "Get home."

He shrugged and drove away.

I thought about going after the Mexicans, but it was still three against one, and I hated to admit it, but that Mustang could blow the doors off my Nova. What the hell did they want with me keys? Had they come all the way to Coyote Crossing to steal my Nova? That would make them the world's worst car thieves.

I went inside the station and cranked the radio. I tried to raise the chief, and when that failed I tried Billy or anyone at all. This was bullshit. Somebody was always supposed to be on duty, either here or listening on the scanner at home. I flipped over to a couple of other channels we used and tried calling all the same people. Nothing. Where the hell was everybody?

I suddenly wanted to feel the weight of my revolver on my belt real bad. I went out to the Nova and fetched my gun, paused when I heard an engine. Maybe a street over. Maybe two streets. Sounded like a big V-8. I got back inside and sat at the desk, swung out the revolver's cylinder. Just as I thought, no bullets.

I opened the top drawer. Fished around for a box of .38 caliber.

I pushed back from the desk when I heard the big engine again, closer this time. I didn't doubt it was the Mustang. I went to the window, peeked through the blinds but couldn't see anything. I went through the back room and opened the door to the alley, stood there a moment listening. Quiet.

The alley stank like trash. It was still so damn hot. I stepped out, looked up and down, trying to catch any little hint of movement in the shadows. I didn't hear or see anything, but then a light in the firehouse window caught my eye. Wasn't supposed to be anyone in there, although the town council certainly wouldn't feel the need to inform me if they were doing some work on the place. What kind of work at this time of night, I couldn't guess.

I should probably take a look. I was wearing a badge after all, and they hadn't fired me yet.

I went back inside and grabbed the revolver off the desk, clipped it to my belt. Okay, let's see what's in the firehouse. I headed down the alley, my hand resting on the revolver. My own breathing sounded a little too loud in my ears.

Simmer down, dumbass.

I listened at the backdoor of the fire station. All I heard was dead wood. I tried the knob. Unlocked. I swung it in, waiting for the hinges to creak, but they didn't. I entered a kitchen, florescent lights buzzing overhead. I expected the place to smell musty and unused, but it didn't.

I paused, surveyed the kitchen counter. Unopened cans of beans. A big stack of paper plates. Jugs of supermarket water. Had the state passed the new budget? Maybe the firefighters were moving back in. I wondered if that meant there wouldn't be enough in the budget to put me on full time. Like it mattered anyway. I was sure Krueger would take my star away in the morning.

I walked through the kitchen, down a short hall and found another door which lead into the garage. I cracked the door and looked inside. The lights were on, and a truck was parked there. A big moving van. The words *Budget*

Movers still showed through where they had been painted over. Somebody had taped over the little windows of the garage door to keep the light from showing on the street.

I heard movement and held my breath. Voices.

The door crack didn't let me see too much, but I wasn't ready to barge in yet. I shifted around, strained to see and hear. A couple of guys standing in back of the truck, mostly out of sight. The elbow and leg of one just in view. A black shirt and jeans. I closed my eyes, put my ear to the door crack.

The first voice was probably in English but with such a thick Spanish accent, I couldn't follow what he was saying. The other voice was clearer and in English. I held my breath, strained to listen.

Billy.

It was Billy's voice, and I could almost hear what he was saying. The two seemed to be arguing, but it wasn't too heated. Nothing too passionate, just a disagreement about something or other. But since I just had my ass stomped by some Mexicans, you can bet your sweet ass I was curious what Deputy Billy was doing in a supposedly closed up firehouse, talking to a Mexican, hell, maybe even the guys who'd kicked me in the ribs.

So yeah, I was going top find out more.

I opened the door just enough to scoot through then shut it back. I crouch-walked to the front of the truck, put a hand on the hood. Cold. It had been parked here a little while, or anyway, it hadn't just arrived. I eased my way down the other side where there was a narrow aisle between the truck and a bunch of oil cans and tools and other stuff that had collected up against the wall. I went on my belly by the rear tire, lay there flat and stone still, trying to control my breathing.

"I told you these ain't even the right ones." Billy's voice. Exasperated. The jangle sound of keys. "I tried every one of them three times."

"You said get the keys from him and I did," insisted the heavily accented Mexican.

"Hell, you probably got the keys to that piece of shit Nova."

Now that was just fucking uncalled for.

The Mexican muttered something I didn't catch. They talked so damn fast.

"You better watch your Goddamn mouth," Billy said. "This isn't my fault, remember? You people are the ones fucked this up. Where the hell is Juanita, anyway?"

The Mexican said something again, talking too low to catch.

"Good then," Billy said. "Keep her out of the way and go find the boy again and get the right keys this time."

Mumbling.

"Yes, right now, Goddamn it. We got to get this shit back on the rails."

The Mexican mumbled one more time and walked back toward the door I'd just come through. I watched his steps under the truck and recognized the boots. I'd seen one of them up close, standing square on my chest. I wasn't eager for a replay of that situation.

The door slammed shut, and the Mexican was gone.

Billy shuffled his feet and said, "Shit."

Okay, time for me to back the fuck out of there and call in the Marines.

I backed right into a stack of oil cans. They tumbled and clattered across the cement. Son of a bitch! Just like some dumb shit in a Three Stooges movie.

"Who's there?" Billy came around the truck.

I stood up quick, tried and failed to look casual.

"Toby." Billy's face got hard like I'd never seen before. "How long you been there? What did you hear?"

"Just saw the light on, thought I'd better check it out." I tried to play it cool but couldn't stop my head from looking around for an escape route. "But I guess you got everything under control here."

He took two real slow steps toward me. "I told you to go home, Toby."

"Yeah."

"We're … uh … hiring some guys to fix up the fire-house," Billy said.

"That Mexican and two of his buddies just kicked my ass."

Billy shook his head. "No, not this guy. You're think-ing of somebody else."

"No I'm not."

"I said you're thinking of somebody else," Billy said. "You need to trust me on this."

"I *just* saw the guy, man."

"Jesus, Toby, you're not making this easy. You could play along, you know."

"What are you talking about?" I asked.

"It's a shame. A damn crying shame, but there's a whole lot of shit going on here that isn't any of your busi-ness, and you'll mess it up if I let you blab it around."

I forced a laugh. It sounded scared. "Blab what, man? I don't know what you're talking about. I won't blab."

"Uh-huh." He reached for the fire axe hanging on the wall, hefted it, testing the weight.

I thought this real quick: Billy wasn't wearing his gun. I was.

My hand fell to my holster, but it was a bad play. Billy was already on me, the axe coming down fast. I threw up my hands to catch the handle as Billy barreled into me. We tumbled back into the oil cans and tools, something hard digging into my back, but I didn't let go of the axe.

He sat on my chest, put all his weight into the axe. The blade hovered over my nose and edged closer. I cocked my head to the side and lifted up, opened my mouth wide as I could and bit into his knuckles. He hollered. Blood sprayed hot and salty into my mouth. He hung onto the axe, so I bit harder, grinding the teeth in until I hit bone.

Billy howled into a screech and let go, blood splashing over the two of us like an exploded ketchup packet. I spit out a wad of flesh then shoved the axe. The flat of the blade caught him good on the chin, and he tumbled off me.

I stood and ran, still clutching the axe to my chest.

A hand grabbed my ankle. I went flying, landing hard on the floor.

I scrambled to one knee, turned in time to see Billy coming at me again, full-blown murder in his eyes. I swept out one handed, the axe biting into Billy's shin. He grunted and went down right in front of me. I stood, swung the axe over my head. Billy looked up, his eyes blinking wide with terror a split-second before the axe bounced off his skull, the strike vibrating up through my arms, a shock of pain in my wrists.

A slash down his forehead fountained blood. He screamed and screamed and screamed. I swung the axe again, and it lodged deep in the side of his neck. More blood. I'd never seen so much.

Billy sprawled flat on his back, his whole body twitching like he was being electrocuted. It seemed to go on forever, his legs kicking out, hands shaking. Finally he settled down, eyes wide open to nothing.

I flung myself on the garage door, fumbled with the latch. My face was burning up. I couldn't breathe. I got it open, raised it and stumbled out to the street, gulping air. I went to my knees and puked. Cold sweat blossomed on my forehead, and I started shivering.

My head swam. I gave myself a moment, breathed in through the nose and out through the mouth. I didn't want to see or hear anything, didn't want to think. I just wanted to kneel there with my eyes closed until the world stopped spinning. When I felt settled enough, I went back inside the firehouse.

I went through Billy's pockets and retrieved Roy's keys. Then I fished another set out of my pocket, not my own keys but those belonging to the late Luke Jordan. The back of the truck was locked with a padlock. I tried three keys and the fourth one fit.

This time I planned to be ready. I pulled my revolver.

I slowly lifted the latch. I took a deep breath, mentally counted one, two, three, and threw the truck door open.

A swarm of Mexicans ran over me. The sudden silence erupted with yelling and shouts in Spanish. I yelled too, backed away, panicked. I jerked the trigger at the mass of bodies coming at me. *Click. Click. Click.*

I hadn't loaded the gun.

They bumped and shoved as they ran past. I screamed. But they went around me, flooding through the open garage door, and they were all out on Main Street now, maybe forty of them. Mostly men, but some women too, and I think I saw a child. The night was alive with the chatter of Spanish in the air. I got caught up, found myself standing in front of the firehouse, the Mexicans melting into the night like a fistful of brown pebbles tossed into a dark river.

CHAPTER SEVEN

The racket of fleeing Mexicans faded, and I stood again in the hot still night. I blinked into the darkness, forcing my heartbeat down to something human. They'd gone off in every direction. I wouldn't have known how to start rounding them up even if I'd wanted to. I went back in, looked at Billy's corpse. I pulled out my Winstons with shaking hands, lit one and smoked.

I always wondered if I'd have to kill somebody one day, but I never thought it would be Billy, or anyone I knew, anyone I worked with. Once, I was in this fight in a little shithole lounge outside Amarillo. The place got out of hand, and we tried to stay out of it, but some of these motherfuckers got up on the stage and this big biker got a hold on our drummer. The drummer was a little scrawny guy, and I could see that biker was about to break him into a dozen pieces.

I swung my guitar as hard as I could, and the crack on the biker's skull was so loud, it stopped the rest of the fight, everybody looking up to the stage as this beefy son of a bitch went flopping off the stage, blood pouring into his eyes. I was scared then, worried I'd killed the guy. I checked the hospital three days in a row until I heard he was going to be okay, and then I hauled my ass out of town.

But there wasn't any power on Earth going to bring Billy back. There was an axe lodged in his neck, and I'd put it there. Billy's wife was a red-haired woman with freckles named Cindy. She taught fifth grade. I tried to remember if they had a kid or not and then very quickly stopped trying to remember.

Don't think about it.

I heard somebody clear his throat, and I spun quickly, my hands going to the revolver on my belt. Never mind it didn't have any bullets.

The Mexican loitering in the frame of the garage door was short and dark, broad flat nose. Black hair down past his neck. He wore dirty jeans and a stained undershirt. Sandals. He held up his hands like *whoa, pal. No trouble here*. He pointed at my cigarette, motioned with two fingers at his mouth.

I held the pack out to him, like I was trying to lure a squirrel with a crust of bread. He approached slowly, took one from the pack. He made a thumb flicking motion for a light, and I sparked him up with my Bic. I backed up to a big toolbox, used it as a bench and lit a new Winston for myself. My hands still shook, but not quite so bad.

My new pal squatted in front of me, puffed, looked around the firehouse. His gaze landed on dead Billy. He muttered Spanish, offered me a sheepish smile and a shrug as if to say *Sometimes you just have to put an axe though a guy.*

He finished the cigarette, stood, uselessly dusted off his pants. I took some more cigarettes from the pack and handed them to him. "For the road."

"*Muchas gracias.*" He took the smokes and headed for the door.

I watched him shamble away with nothing but the clothes on his back, probably nothing in his pockets either. No I.D. maybe. Where would he go first? What would he do? How would he eat? The answers were all too likely.

"Hold on," I called after him.

He paused, raised an eyebrow.

"Don't do anything in town, okay? Take your show on the road."

He looked blank.

"Don't steal anything," I said. "Don't break into anyone's house. At least wait until you get to the next town."

His blank look got more blank.

I tapped the star on my chest. "*Policia.*" I put my hand on the pistol, looked him square in the eye. "I don't want any trouble from you." I thumbed the badge again. "Just move on someplace else."

Understanding dawned in his eyes, and he nodded vigorously. "*Si, si.*" He jogged away.

Good. Maybe he'd cause trouble somewhere else. Maybe he wouldn't cause any at all. He probably didn't have a nickel or a plan, but somehow I envied him, running off into the night with two cigarettes and a clean slate. I hoped he wouldn't hurt anybody. I had bigger worries.

I stood, flicked away the cigarette butt, and closed the big garage door, made sure it was latched. I approached the back of the moving van, and was almost knocked over by the stink. I had the idea that maybe I'd get in there and have a looksee, find clues or whatever bullshit real cops do, but the combination of urine, crap and body odor was like some kind of impenetrable force-field. I shut the door, clapped the padlock back on.

I stood over Billy again, looked into his vacant eyes, knew I had to go get somebody about this. Fact is I did toy with the notion of hauling the body off and burying it, pretending like the whole thing never happened. *What? Who? Billy?* Shrug. *Haven't seen him. Why? Something wrong?*

No, that shit never works out. Never. I'd seen enough CSI shows to know that, and anyway I was spattered pretty good with Billy's blood. No, this was a big, fat mess which wasn't going to go away or clean up easy.

I left the firehouse through the kitchen and walked the alley back to the police station. Inside, I tried the chief on the radio again and came up empty. I was starting to worry something bad had happened to him. Billy had tried to kill me. What else might he have been capable of?

I flipped open the Rolodex on the chief's desk and dialed Amanda's number. Her machine picked up after six rings. Her recording sounded very businesslike. I waited for the beep.

"Uh, Amanda, this is Toby. I think ... uh ... listen, we got a problem, and I need somebody to get down here to the station. I'll try Karl next." I hung up, wondering how much of a dork I sounded like. I hated talking to those things.

I sighed, thought about waiting five minutes then trying Amanda again. I did not want to call Karl, former Sooner linebacker, loud-mouth, muscle-head prick. He blew out his knee at University of Oklahoma, came back to Coyote Crossing and stayed. Putting on a badge made him feel like big man on campus again, I guess. He also volunteered as assistant football coach for the school's JV team. He enjoyed shouting at people.

I suspected he basically looked at me like some guitar-playing pussy. I'd never gotten any warm vibes from him.

Anyway, it didn't matter. I couldn't deal with this shit myself, so I dialed Karl's number.

After three rings I heard him pick up, some kind of rattle, a cough and a moan, Karl's jock voice asking, "What the hell time is it?"

"It's Toby, Karl. I need you to get down to the station. There's been … trouble."

"What the hell are you talking about, man?"

"Just get down here, okay? I can't handle this, and I don't want to explain it all on the phone."

"Where's Krueger?"

"I can't find the chief. That's why I'm calling you."

A big sigh on his end, lips smacking. "Okay just … let me get dressed. Just stay there, right?"

"Okay."

"Shit." He hung up.

I wasn't sure if I felt better or not, but at least it was out of my hands. Karl's problem now. I wondered if he'd arrest me, what the procedure was. Then it occurred to me Karl and Billy were pretty tight pals. Maybe Karl wouldn't arrest me at all.

Maybe he'd pull his gun and blow my brains out.

CHAPTER EIGHT

I put my feet up on the desk, sat back and lit another Winston. I was going through the pack pretty fast. I wasn't really supposed to smoke inside the station, but if you kill a guy you get some slack. I was pretty sure that was a rule.

I exhaled, watched the smoke twist and drift, and replayed the conversation between Billy and the Mexican back at the firehouse. There was something I was supposed to pay attention to, something important, but I couldn't get it straight in my head.

I patted my pockets. Three sets of keys. Mine, Roy's and Luke Jordan's.

Keys.

I picked up the phone and dialed. It rang, three times, four, five. *Come on, come on come on …*

Billy's words came back to me all to clear. *Go find the boy again and get the right keys this time.*

Eight rings, nine, ten. *Answer the damn phone, Doris!*

I slammed the phone down. This time I didn't rush off. I took the box of .38 ammunition, loaded my revolver, stuck the rest of the box in my pants pocket. I was out the front door in a flash, getting into the Nova and cranking the engine. I gunned it, squealed my tires making a U-turn on Main and hauled ass west of town, the gas pedal stomped flat.

It was all too easy to imagine. Her on the floor dead while they sacked the place looking for the keys. Or maybe they'd do worse than kill her. Who could say? Anything. And the boy. I edged forward in my seat, strained against the safety belt, willing the Nova to go faster. The engine screamed so loud I thought it would explode any minute.

I slowed as I approached the trailer park entrance and killed the lights. I parked half a block away then headed for my trailer with my revolver out. No lights in the windows. I tried to make my heartbeat slow, and I told myself a little story about how Doris probably just went back to bed and was too lazy to answer the phone. I scanned the driveway and both sides of the trailer but didn't see the Mustang or any other cars.

I didn't see Doris's car either.

When my boot hit the middle step up to the door, the creak was so loud it made me wince. I held my breath, but nothing happened. I tried to turn the knob. Locked. I stuck the key in and turned slowly. I swung the door open quietly an inch at a time, stepped in, closed the door easy behind me without a loud click.

The revolver felt sweaty and heavy in my hand. I wanted to be ready, but I didn't want to blast Doris by mistake. I stood a long time listening. It seemed like a long time, but it was probably only ten seconds. My mouth felt dry and cottony.

A flickering white light from the living room, dim and twitchy, jagged shadows on the wall and ceiling. I eased down the hall, gun in front of me, rounded the corner and saw the television turned onto a station of white noise. There was a rectangle in the middle of the TV screen, and when I took two steps closer, I saw it was a piece of notebook paper scotch-taped to the screen.

I peeled it off and flipped on the nearest lamp.

It was a note. From Doris.

Toby,

I can't do this anymore. I do not love you, and I don't think I ever did, although I wish I did because you're a good father and a good person. But this just isn't me. I have to get out. If you won't come, then I'll go it alone. I'll send money for the boy once I'm set up in Houston. Don't hate me. It's no use, so please just don't hate me. I knew you'd be

home soon, so I left the boy sleeping--

I knocked over the lamp and end table when I jumped up and ran for my son's room. I burst through the door, stood panting over his crib.

He lay sleeping, the covers completely kicked off. Fresh diaper, Bob the Builder t-shirt halfway up his chest, showing off his perfect round belly. His mouth hung open, his bottom lip looking like pink porcelain. A faint blush on his cheeks.

I set my revolver on his dresser and scooped him up, didn't care if I woke him. I needed to feel his weight against my chest, touch the thin hair on his head. He didn't wake, just made a little toddler noise and wormed his head into my armpit. I backed into the rocking chair, shifted until he was comfortable in my arms. One of his pudgy hands rested on my chest. He felt so warm and solid.

I felt that ache behind my eyes I always get when I'm about to cry. I held it back. No time. Not now. Some kind of relief. An emotional release. But not now. I let it turn to anger.

All I could think was *Bitch. Goddamn bitch*. How could she run off and leave him like that? Our son. My boy. Anything could have happened. When he was eight months old, I came home from a shift, walked past Doris watching Montel on the couch and found the boy in the kitchen. He sat in the playpen, face going blue. I grabbed him, panicked, flipped him upside down and slapped his back until the grape popped out. They say grapes and chunks of hotdog are the two biggest culprits for toddler choking. They'll stick anything into their mouths. I remember my mom pulling a dry bean out of my nostril once.

Doris had felt so bad, I hadn't yelled at her about it. But now all I could think was *Just figures. Goddamn bitch. Fucking stupid bitch*! And I almost cried again.

It occurred to me a second later that she hadn't just abandoned the boy. She'd left me too. Her letter was a crumpled ball in my fist. I smoothed it out, let my eyes adjust to the dim glow of the boy's nightlight, and picked up where I left off.

```
I knew you'd be home soon, so I left the boy
sleeping in his room. He was wet, so I
changed him. There is enough diapers and
milk until the weekend, but then you'll
need to get to the store. I don't know how to
make you understand that I can't stay here
anymore. I thought there was a reason to but
there is not and if I don't go, I'll go crazy.
The Indian woman's name is Alice. I know you
```

always forget. She can watch TJ sometimes. I
will send some money to help when I get a
job in Houston, but I'm not coming back. I
just read what I wrote and I guess I haven't
explained a damn thing. All I can say is
that the more I'd say the less happy you'd
be, so there it is.

Doris

Fuck you, Doris.

I hugged the boy closer to my chest, rocked gently. Now what? Just what the hell was I going to do now? I'd have to talk to the Indian woman. Alice. And I'd have to go soon—tomorrow—to the fertilizer plant. I'd need to earn enough to feed us and keep the lights on and pay Alice when I was working.

Maybe I should have given in to Doris. Gone to Houston. That line of thought pissed me off again. I realized I was rocking too fast, made myself slow down. When TJ was an infant, I'd rock too fast and make him spit up. I'd learned everything, how fast to rock him, how to change him, what he ate.

I suddenly hated the whole fucking unfair world. I'd pawned my guitar and amp so long ago, I couldn't remember what the strings felt like beneath my fingers. I could barely recall playing in some hot, smoky joint, really getting into the groove, how we could mesmerize a crowd when everything was working right. I left all that behind me to do the right thing. Doris was gone, and Molly would leave soon. Was there anything left to sacrifice?

The dried blood on my hands looked black in the pale light. The boy's skin glowing white and untainted. A lifetime of bruises and broken bones waited for him. He'd climb trees and fall out and step on sharp rocks in the river. But it wouldn't keep him out of trees or out of the river. I'd see to that. I didn't want him growing up afraid to live. This was my new mission in life. To make things right for the boy and fuck Doris and everyone else.

Then I remembered I'd axed Billy. Who would take care of TJ if I went to prison? I wanted to cry again.

A noise from outside, the loud creak of the metal step leading up to the back door.

I held my breath and waited, listening. If it was Doris coming back, I'd rip her a new one like she wouldn't believe. I waited, but nobody came inside.

I stood, edged forward and took my revolver from the dresser. The boy slept, a warm and heavy bundle in the crook of my arm. I walked out of TJ's room, stepping softly toward the back door. The bathroom was opposite the door, so I backed in, keeping the revolver trained on the door, listening carefully.

Maybe it was Doris coming back. I wanted to think it was her feeling bad for running off, but she'd have put her key in and opened the door by now. She'd have come in.

The silence was like a thick syrup that had oozed down over the whole trailer. I couldn't hear the step creak or the boy's breathing or any cars out on the highway. Nothing at all. Time held me in the frozen blue haze of my imagination, hoping it was Doris, knowing it wasn't, somebody standing out there waiting to come into my home.

Then, two things at once.

A light rattle from the other side of the trailer. Somebody trying the knob on the front door.

And the middle step at the back door creaked again.

I lifted the revolver and fired, squeezed off three rapid shots.

The bangs shook the trailer, the slugs blasting through the door in a neat triangle. TJ came instantly awake, screaming bloody murder and clutching at my shirt. Something on the back steps went tumble and thud.

Shouts outside, in Spanish.

I ran down the hall, and a blaze of bullets ripped through the trailer, tearing through the walls like they were aluminum foil. I dove for the floor, twisted at the last second to land on my back and avoid crushing the boy. He screamed louder. I hunched over him turtle style, more bullets shredding the trailer, some kind of hellfire machine-gun rattle outside the trailer. The gunfire obliterated a lamp, blasted the television, battered the clock off the wall.

The next burst of fire shattered the living room windows. If they were out front, then I sure as hell was going out the back.

I crawled on two knees and one elbow toward the back door. I held TJ hysterical in the other arm. I stood, revolver ready, and kicked the back door open just as I heard somebody do the same to the front.

I jumped down the three steps and landed next to a dead Mexican in a red shirt, the one who'd kicked me in the ribs, I think. Good.

I ran. Lights came on in some of the other mobile homes, dogs barking insanity. Halfway to the Nova, I turned, looked back at the trailer. A face appeared in the back door. I paused and squeezed off two shots, and the face ducked back inside.

By the time I reached the Nova I saw the Mustang parked right behind me. I shot one of the front tires and the boy jumped in my arms. He was gulping air now, big sobs wracking his whole body. I would never forgive myself. No matter what happened from now forward, I had failed. No child should ever have to go through this.

I got into the Nova and cranked the engine, fishtailed

a U-turn and squealed the tires putting the trailer behind me. More gun shots but growing distant. I remembered Doris had TJ's car seat in her car.

Fuckingbitchfuckingbitchfuckingbitchfuckingbitch…

"D-daddy." He was reaching for me, eyes so blurred with tears he couldn't see.

I pulled him into my lap, kissed the top of his head. "You're going to be okay, buddy. It's going to be okay." He rested his head against my chest, still crying but more evenly, not so panicked and out of control.

I uttered some kind of brief prayer. I wasn't sure about my relationship with God. I was in eighth grade the last time I went to the Methodist Church with my mother. But now seemed like a good time to take it up again. I asked for help. I made promises. I hoped He was listening.

I left the trailer park, drove straight and fast toward town and didn't see anything in the rearview mirror.

CHAPTER NINE

I parked in front of Molly's house, behind her dad's Peterbilt.

I rocked the boy in my arms until he quieted down some. I didn't like what I was about to do. This wasn't really Molly's thing, but I trusted her to be a good person when all was said and done. And I didn't exactly have a whole lot of choices.

I climbed her front steps, the boy on one hip, and knocked. It took a while, and I knocked again. Molly wasn't going to get much sleep tonight. I worried briefly that Roy might've snuck home after I left. I'd shoot him. Swear to God, I would shoot him.

But Roy wasn't home. The door swung open, and Molly stood there in panties and a t-shirt. She rubbed her eyes.

"I need help, Molly."

"What?"

I pushed in past her.

She closed the door. "Is that Toby Junior?"

She'd never seen the boy. They'd both been in my life so thick, it hadn't occurred to me how separate they were. Of course she'd never seen him. "Yes. He's had a scare."

She looked me over. "What happened to you?"

"I'm in a lot of trouble, Molly."

"Tell me."

"I killed Billy Banks." She'd hear about it soon enough anyway.

She gasped, her hand going to her mouth.

"It was self defense," I said too quickly.

"Why?"

"I think Billy was smuggling illegals. Or working with some Mexicans. I don't know. You remember that news story a few years ago, the truck with all those dead illegal aliens in the back? Earlier tonight I found a truck just like that, padlock on the back to keep them inside. Parked in the firehouse."

"No fucking way. They were dead?"

"No, not dead. Live ones."

"Why here?"

"Beats me. You got any milk?"

"I think so."

"Can you warm it up and bring me a cup?" I sat on her couch, held the boy. He wouldn't let go of me, kept shivering.

"I'll put it in the microwave."

"No, you're not supposed to do that. Can you heat it in a pan?"

"Give me a minute." She went to the kitchen.

I rocked the boy in my arms, something overwhelmed him, shock or exhaustion maybe because I watched his eyelids sink down. His cheeks were tear-smeared. In a moment he breathed steadily, back to sleep. I could not imagine holding my head up among decent people if I let anything happen to him. I was supposed to be a dad.

I settled him down on the couch, made a ring of cushions around him, then went into the kitchen. Molly had four different size pans on the counter, her head stuck in the refrigerator.

"We don't have any milk," Molly said. "There's Mellow Yellow and carrot juice."

"It's okay. He's asleep. But we'll need milk in the morning."

"Morning?"

"I need your help, Molly."

Her eyes went round. "Oh, no. I don't know anything about kids."

"I have to go back out there. I can't take the boy. He has to be someplace safe, okay? I trust you."

"Come on, Toby. There's got to be some old lady you know who can do it. I've never even been a baby sitter."

"Molly, look at me. There's serious shit going on."

"I can't. I've never even changed a diaper."

I put a hand on each of her shoulders. "Molly, I'm begging you. Look at me. Please. I'm begging you."

"Okay, okay. Crap. I don't know what he eats or anything."

She was right. I'd fled the trailer without the diaper bag. No wipes or diapers or ass cream. Nothing. It wasn't like dropping off a stray kitten. The boy needed things.

"I'll make a run to the store. I'll get diapers. I need you to do this."

"I'll do it, but what if he gets sick or—"

"He'll just sleep. It'll be fine."

She sighed.

I took her into my arms, felt relieved when she hugged me back. Her head tilted up and I bent to kiss her, felt her tongue slip into my mouth, one of her warm hands on my neck. We let it go on like that for a while. I didn't want to leave, but knew I had to. I slipped out of her arms, stepped away.

"I'll be back with diapers and milk. Soon."

I paused on the way out, touched TJ's head. I hoped he hadn't been traumatized. I hoped he'd sleep peaceful and have good dreams and not wake up asking for Mommy. I made silent promises to him.

Outside, I hopped in the Nova, lit a Winston and headed for the Texaco.

CHAPTER TEN

I was halfway down the Six back to the Texaco when fatigue sat on my chest like a five hundred pound gorilla. So tired. The night had rubbed me raw, the adrenaline leaking away, leaving me feeling wrung out. I almost nodded off at the wheel, slapped my own face to keep awake.

I pulled into the Texaco, went inside.

The same girl was on duty. She looked tired too. She opened her mouth to say something but thought better of it after getting an eyeful of me. I didn't even want to think what I looked like.

I grabbed a half-gallon of milk, a pack of diapers, wipes and three energy drinks, took it all to the counter. The girl rang it up, and it came to like a million dollars. Fucking convenience store prices. I had my wallet this time and paid.

Back in the Nova I popped open one of the energy drinks. It tasted like melted cough drops and propane. I saw these high school kids all over town drinking them all the time. What the hell was going on with their taste buds? I made myself drink the whole thing then started the car and headed back to Coyote Crossing.

The drink kicked in a mile from town, like triple caffeine pulsing through my veins. Eyes open wide. I felt the juice humming through my veins. I drummed the steering wheel in time to Golden Earring. It wasn't usually my kind of music, but my old band had done a really twisted, kick-ass cover of this song, so I let it play. A lot of these old bands weren't so bad. I flew through the night wired on the energy drink, the music lifting the car through space and time. The full moon hung yellow in the sky like the devil's cream pie.

I caught sight of them in the rearview mirror a split-second before the Mustang slammed into the back of the Nova.

I swerved, the two right tires going off the road and kicking up dust. I jerked the wheel, got the Nova back in the center. They'd blazed up behind me hard and fast with the lights off. They bumped me again, and I heard the tinkle-crunch of the back end dying. The rear bumper went clanging down the highway.

Motherfucker!

I stomped the gas. I might as well have been trying to escape on a Big Wheel. The Mustang slammed me again hard. I guessed they might be pissed at having to change a tire. They switched on the headlights and I winced at the brights. On the next slam, I lost control, the Nova spinning in the road, the Mustang's headlights a bright blur across my windshield. I ended up pointed the opposite direction, hands white-knuckled on the wheel and Golden Earring still pounding the speakers.

The Mustang roared past me so close on the driver's side it clipped the mirror with a sharp crack. The motor had stalled, and I turned the key, pumped gas and she fired up again. The Mustang was making a slow turn and coming back.

I fishtailed, pointed the Nova dead into the oncoming headlights and pressed the accelerator until the engine screamed murder. A good old-fashioned game of chicken. Let's see who had the balls and who didn't. Who'd blink first, him or me?

Me.

I wrenched the wheel right as hard as I could, skidding the Nova sideways. This part of the Six was elevated two or three feet, so the shoulder went down at a steep angle. The Nova tilted alarmingly, and I thought I was destined to be upside down. I fought the wheel, every muscle in my body straining, great sprays of dust kicking up on either side as I straightened out and headed back for the highway. I bottomed out as the Nova climbed the shoulder and hit the highway. I got up to speed.

The Mustang's headlights filled the rearview mirror in no time flat.

I thought it was coming up to smash my rear again, but it swerved up alongside and the two cars bumped side to side. I turned the wheel toward him, put a nice dent in his passenger side door, but he came back double-hard and I almost left the road again. He came over, and I slammed the breaks, let him get in front of me.

My turn, asshole.

I gave it the gas before he could get set, and bashed him a good one in the rear end. One of my headlights winked out, but I killed both his tail lights. Score one for the deputy.

My minor triumph didn't last long. He sped up, juked and jived, braked hard and was along side me again. He careened into me hard, and this time I did go off the road, went down the steep embankment, the car started to tilt. I panicked, turned the wheel the wrong way, and the car rolled.

The Nova became a shook-up snow globe of crap, candy wrappers and soda cans and fast-food wrappers flying as the car slid to a stop upside down, the remaining headlight flailing uselessly against the dust cloud which had swallowed the car. I felt like I'd been flung into another reality.

I new they'd be on me soon. I unbuckled the seatbelt, uncrumpled myself. I couldn't get the door open, so I rolled down the window, scrambled out and pulled the revolver. I coughed, blinked against the swirling dust. I wiped at my eyes, something sticking. There was a gash over my left eye, and I smeared the dust and blood across my face. I leaned back against the Nova, kept the gun up, waiting for somebody to come kill me.

Nobody did.

I belly crawled up the embankment, saw what had happened.

Fifty yards away, the Mustang had gone off the road on the other side, its nose over the embankment. It scraped bottom as it rocked back and forth, gunning its engine, trying to unstick itself. The back tires kicked up dirt and rocks. It would rip free any second and come back for me.

I reached back into the Nova and grabbed the bag with the diapers and milk. I began jogging across country back to town. It was less than a mile away, the lights clearly visible. Even with the moon out, they wouldn't be able to spot me across the vast black of the night landscape. Let them hunt for me near the flipped Nova. I jogged a minute and allowed myself a quick look back.

The Mustang was loose again, cruising slowly. It parked more or less near the overturned Nova, the headlights stabbing the night. If I got lucky, maybe they'd piss away a whole hour cruising around the wreck looking for me.

I turned back toward town and kept jogging.

CHAPTER ELEVEN

H oly crap!" Molly muffled herself to a hoarse whisper. "What happened?"

"How's the boy?"

"Still sleeping. Are you going to be okay?"

"It looks worse than it is. Mostly dirt. Let me in please."

She stepped aside, and I handed her the convenience store bag on the way to her bathroom. I looked at myself in the mirror. I wasn't pretty, face a caked mix of blood, dirt and sweat. I filled the sink with cold water, splashed my face. The water stung the cut over my eye. I ignored it, kept splashing until I looked almost human again. I wiped my face on one of Molly's clean towels, smudged it brown and red, tossed it on the floor. I drained the water, turned on the cold tap again and scooped handfuls of water until I got the dirt taste out of my mouth.

I took a leak, flushed.

Molly hovered in the hall, waiting for me to come out.

"Toby, stay here. Every time you go out there, something—"

"I have something to do."

I walked past her and into the kitchen, opened the refrigerator. She'd put my other two energy drinks in there. I took them. There were two chicken legs on a plate. I took them too. Back in the living room, Molly looked at me, frowning with her whole face, arms crossed. I didn't have time to think of anything I could say to make her feel better. I looked at the boy. He was still sleeping. Good.

I went toward the front door.

"Toby, please."

"Molly, just watch TJ, okay? Stay here and watch him."

I left quickly before she could think of anything else to say to me. I went through my pockets until I found the right set of keys. I unlocked Roy's Peterbilt and hauled myself up into the cab. The truck was a fucking monster. I sat, looked over the gearshift and gauges, trying to remember back a few years when I'd driven a pal's big-rig a total of twice just for laughs. I started the engine and cranked the air-conditioning.

The air felt good. I sat there a second, not moving, just letting the air conditioning hit my dirty, sweaty skin.

I sat and ate the chicken legs, tossed the bones out the window. The armrest was also a storage compartment for CDs. I flipped through Roy's music collection with a raised eyebrow. He had Celine Dion, Kenny G, Lionel Richie, Abba Gold, Three Tenors, Sade, Britney Spears, Seal, Clay Aiken ...

Damn, Roy. What the fuck?

I shoved Abba into the CD player, drowned out the opening seconds of "Dancing Queen" grinding the Peterbilt into first gear. The thing finally lurched forward, and I was off and running. I eased out of the residential neighborhood, trying not to flatten mailboxes or picket fences as I went. I made a wide slow turn onto main, found the alley I was looking for the other side of Skeeter's.

I pulled past, then attempted to back in but had to stop before taking out a railing on Skeeter's front deck. I pulled forward and tried again. Five more tries, and I'd cussed every bad word I could think of, but I finally backed the rig into the alley. I killed the lights, but left the engine on with the air conditioner blowing.

I sat and watched Main Street, popped open an energy drink and choked it down. Abba sang "S.O.S." S.O.S. Damn right. Abba wasn't so bad. I would never admit that to a single living soul.

I fished the box of .38 ammo out of my pants pocket and reloaded the revolver. Instead of sliding it back in the holster, I set it on the passenger seat where I could grab it fast. I knew Karl was probably steaming, waiting for me at the stationhouse, but I had something to take care of that just wouldn't wait. And fuck Karl anyway. Just fuck that guy.

Fuck everybody.

Ten minutes crawled by, and I finally saw the Mustang come rolling down Main from the west. I knew he hadn't given up on me, knew he'd come back this way sooner or later. *I knew it, you cocksucker.* Under the street lights, the Mustang looked rough. My upside-down Nova had clearly lost the battle, but the Mustang had taken a pretty good beating. The front was mashed in like somebody had punched the car in the nose, scrapes and dents along the side. The cherry paint job was crusted with dirt and grime.

Good. Fuck you, Ford Mustang Mach 1.

They passed, and I counted to thirty. Then I flipped on the headlights and pulled out of the alley, followed the Mustang. I kept it to the speed limit. If they thought I was up to something, they'd simply hit the gas and fly away.

We headed out of town going east, and I felt sure I knew where they were headed. The Mona Lisa Lodge was the only motel for miles and miles and it was two minutes from Coyote Crossing. I eased up, let the Mustang pull ahead of me. I couldn't let them get too far. Hard to follow with their tail lights out. Blamed myself for that one.

Until they fired me I was the law. But this was about more than that. This was payback. I shifted gears and kept pace. Hell is on your heels, you sons of bitches.

The Mona Lisa's green neon sprouted on the horizon. There wasn't much to the motel. A dozen rooms lined up in a row and a dank office with an ice machine and a Pepsi vending machine. Probably Widow McCarthy on duty at the desk or more likely sleeping one off in the back office. I knew what the inside of the rooms looked like. Plain earth tones, dingy yellow tile in the bathrooms. No pictures on the wall. Two fuzzy channels on the TV. I'd been to the Mona Lisa twice with Molly when her Dad was in town, and we couldn't wait. I'd told Doris I'd picked up a late shift. Molly had told her dad she was sleeping at a friend's.

I wondered if I could convince Molly to stay in Coyote Crossing and marry me. Maybe she would learn to love the boy. That made me laugh. Hell. She probably didn't even love me. Might as well pull the moon from the sky and put it in my pocket. And anyway, I was probably going to jail.

The Mustang pulled into the hotel parking lot, parked in front of the room at the far end of the line. I didn't slow the Peterbilt, drove right on past, just another all night trucker on his way to nowhere, USA.

I made it a quarter mile down the highway, decelerated and made a slow U-turn. I paused in the road, let the truck idle. I lit a cigarette. Let them get comfortable in there, drop their guard.

I headed back for the motel, working my way up through the gears. I thought about killing the headlights but switched on the brights instead. "Waterloo" blasted from the speakers. I hit the Mona Lisa's parking lot full speed, angled myself toward the Mustang.

The Peterbilt plowed into the driver's side with a *pop crunch*, like hitting an empty soda-pop can with a baseball bat. The big-rig pushed the Mustang up on its side, and I shoved it along like that for a second until it bounced out of the way. I headed back for the road, turned for another pass.

Two Mexicans spilled out of the motel room, guns in hands, a guy in red and the honcho in the black shirt. I aimed the rig at their front door and started shifting gears. Kept leaning on the horn. They lifted their pistols.

I blasted the big-rig's horn at them just as they opened fire. Slugs punched through the windshield a foot to my right, spider-webbing the glass. The next shot inched closer, and I hunched in my seat, still shifting and pressing the gas pedal. I didn't quite get up to speed like I'd hoped, but I guess I was making my point because both the Mexicans fled back into the hotel room.

Bad move.

I blasted the horn one more time before the Peterbilt smashed through the door and window, dust and rubble raining down on the rig's windshield. I put it in park and killed the ignition, grabbed the revolver which had slid to the floor and climbed down from the cab. I stumbled on the rubble. An arm in a red sleeve stuck out from under the rig's front tire. I decided I didn't want to see any more.

I got to my feet, slipping on the loose rubble. The rig's headlights stabbed through the swirling dust in the motel room. A figure emerged through the beams of light, like a ghost drifting through the dust cloud. He came closer, and I saw it was the honcho in the black shirt, one hand clutching a pistol, the other wiping at his eyes. He coughed hard, waved the gun in front of him.

I pointed the revolver at him. "Drop the gun, *amigo!*"

He coughed again, blinked the dust out of his eyes. "*Puerco!*"

"I said drop it."

He fired way over my head. I pulled the trigger four times, red blotches sprouting across his chest. He twitched a little before collapsing to his knees, hovered there a moment, then toppled over.

I stood there breathing hard a moment, everything so quiet except the splashing from the bathroom where a pipe had torn loose. The place smelled like cordite and plaster dust and blood and the big-rig's overheated engine. Another smell too, permeating the mix. Somebody's bowels had let go.

I felt nauseated, backed out of the motel room, careful not to trip over rubble. Outside I gulped clean air. The lights were on in the motel office, so I headed that way. I didn't hurry.

Inside at the front desk, Myrtle McCarthy was coming out of the back room, wearing a blue terrycloth robe, rubbing her eyes and putting her glasses on. She got a load of me and flinched. I could smell gin ten steps away.

"You okay, Toby?"

"I'll live, Miss McCarthy. Just wanted to let you know there's been a little trouble. You might want to call your insurance people in the morning."

She looked past me at the big-rig still parked halfway into the motel room. "Hell and blood, how'd that happen?"

"It's a long story, ma'am. I'm afraid those Mexicans are dead."

"The one in the other room too?"

One of my eyebrows went up and made a question mark out of itself. "Other room?"

"They took two rooms right next to each other when they checked in."

"Can you let me have the pass key, ma'am?"

She reached under the counter, came out with a key on a big green keychain, a picture of the Mona Lisa on it. She hesitated a second before handing it over.

I took the key. "I'll be right back."

I walked back down the line of rooms, a little faster this time. There were no lights on in the room next to the one I'd wrecked. I put the key in, turned the knob and went in fast at a crouch.

The room shook with two quick pops of gunfire, white flashes form the center of the darkness. The bullets chewed plaster off the wall an inch from my face. I went low, fired twice without aiming. When I squeezed the trigger a third time, I heard *click*.

"Fuck!"

I tossed the revolver away and threw myself in the direction of the flashes. Another shot went off, and I felt the heat of the blast on my face. I barreled into a body and we both went over. The guy was smaller than I expected. I ended up on top, punched down as hard as I could, felt and heard the smack of flesh. I punched again. I felt for his hands, found the pistol and grabbed it.

I stood, panting, backed up against the wall and flipped on the light switch. The gun in my hand was a silver .25 automatic. A little, inaccurate piece of crap. You'd need to shove the thing straight up your target's nose to hit anything. I looked at my opponent and saw I'd just punched the shit out of a woman. My mother would have been disappointed. I wouldn't lose any sleep. The bitch had tried to shoot me, after all.

She was a light skinned Mexican, maybe twenty-nine or thirty years old, big wads of brown hair piled on her head, messed up a little from sleeping. I figured she'd been in bed since she wore only black panties. Her breasts stood up for themselves, big but not drooping, thin waist, long legs. She worked herself into a crouch, then stood slowly, keeping her eyes on me the whole time, like a cat trying to decide between fight or flight.

I kept her own automatic pointed at her chest, retrieved my revolver and shoved it back in the holster.

We looked at each other a few seconds. I didn't exactly know what to do with her.

"Are you going to arrest me now, cowboy?" One side of her mouth curled into a sly smile. She had only a light accent.

"You are so fucking under arrest."

She trailed a finger under one of her breasts. "Like this? You're going to take me in naked?"

"Get something on. You reach for anything other than clothes, and I'll unload this toy pistol on you."

She did it slowly, like she wasn't bothered at all. She slipped a cottony dress with a tight floral pattern over her head, stepped into a pair of stringy sandals.

She held out her hands. "You want to cuff me."

I didn't have any cuffs, but I mumbled out the Miranda rights. I'd memorized them, had even practiced them in front of a mirror.

I'd killed at least four men that I knew of, but she was the first person in my career as a deputy that I'd ever arrested.

CHAPTER TWELVE

The big-rig made a hell of a racket backing out over the rubble, scraping bottom, getting caught up on whatever I didn't care to think about. The rig stalled, and I cranked it again, fought to get the thing into gear.

"Are you sure you know how to drive one of these?" She sat in the passenger seat, legs crossed, her hands bound by a power cord I'd ripped from a lamp.

I ignored her, bullied the truck into first gear and headed back to town. There was a pretty bad rattle somewhere under the hood and a grinding sound coming from the brakes. Roy would be pissed. Tough shit.

"What is my charge?" she asked.

"What?"

"You have to charge me with something if you arrest me."

I thought about that a second. "Well, you shot at me for starters."

"You broke into my room. Self defense."

"Aiding and abetting the smuggling of illegal aliens. That specific enough for you?" I popped a Winston into my mouth and lit it.

"I don't know what you are talking about."

"Sure you don't. You talk better English than the others."

"I went to University of Texas El Paso for an accounting degree."

"Hey, I bet you're in charge of the smuggling. The ring leader. Big boss."

"They don't let women be in charge of anything where I come from. Can I have one of those?"

I leaned over and stuck a cigarette in her mouth, lit it for her.

"I want a lawyer," she said.

That made me crack up laughing. Hard.

"This cord is too tight around my wrists."

"Get used to it."

She frowned. "Stupid redneck cowboy. You are in far over your head."

"Oh yeah?"

"Yes. Soon you will see." She smirked, puffed the Winston.

"You know what I think? I think you shook that sweet little ass of yours in front of Luke Jordan and got him killed. Who did it? Your boyfriend maybe. Who's your boyfriend, Miss Thing? That honcho in the fancy black shirt, I'm guessing."

"He's my brother."

"He's dead."

And that shut her up pretty good and quick.

I parked the rig in front of the stationhouse, hauled in the Mexican gal by the elbow. I was hoping Karl would be there, but the place was empty. I untied her and shoved her into one of the holding cells.

"Wait." She came to the front of the cell, grabbed the bars and pinned me with a hard stare. "Did you mean it? He's dead?"

"Yes." I didn't feel like rubbing it in, but I didn't apologize either.

Her hand shot out, and she raked me across the face with her nails.

I jumped back, the flesh on my left cheek stinging.

"I will kill you," she shrieked. "If it's the last thing I do, I will see you writhing on the ground in agony. I will put a knife in your belly!" Her face was a mask of wild, animal rage.

"Lady, shut up."

I slumped at the desk, found a box of tissue and began dabbing at my fresh scratches. She kept cursing at me in

Mexican. She seemed pretty earnest about whatever she was saying.

I reloaded my revolver again and stuck the woman's little automatic in my belt.

I picked up the phone to call Molly, but it was dead. I checked the line, made sure it was plugged into the wall. I went into the back room and tried the phone hanging on the wall next to the lockers. It was dead too.

Hell.

I didn't know if this was a bad sign or just bad luck. Last year a giant thunderstorm had swept through the county and a lighting bolt had fried the main telephone juncture box for the whole town. Nobody could make a call for three days, and the town was too far out in the middle of Butt-Fuck Egypt for cell phones to work. Christ. Of all the times for the phone to go dead. I slumped against the lockers, rubbed my eyes.

It was nice and quiet in the back room away from the Mexican hellcat. I sat on the edge of the safe and finished my cigarette. There was probably some paperwork to fill out when you arrested somebody. A report. I didn't even know the woman's name.

I went back out front, stood in front of her cell. "Hey, what's your name?"

She cursed in Spanish and spat at me.

"Oh, come on."

The stationhouse door creaked open behind me and Karl walked in. Thank God. Karl was a giant jock prick, but now I could dump this whole mess into his lap. There was a good chance he'd whip some Miranda on me and I'd be in the next cell along side the hellcat, but at this point I just wanted to be done with it.

"Where the hell you been?" Karl said.

Karl was a good six inches taller than me and twice as wide, square chin like a block of granite, a hawkish nose that filled up his face. His hair was a dirty brown buzz cut. Teeth like a horse's. He smelled like Aqua Velva.

He growled at me. "I've been here twice after you called. So what the hell is the big, fat emergency that you were all worried …" His gaze drifted past me to the Mexican lady in the cell. "Oh … shit."

I turned back to the hellcat. "You can try your luck spitting at him for a while." I turned my head to look back at Karl. "I guess I'd better explain—"

The fist hit me square between the eyes, and my head snapped back and bounced off the bars of the cell. I staggered, took another punch in the jaw, and my knees went rubbery. The room tilted, went blurry and my face bounced off the floor.

There was an angry buzzing in my ears, and my vision went hot red before fading to darkness.

CHAPTER THIRTEEN

I blinked, shook my head and tried to clear the cobwebs. Someone was slapping my face.

"Wake up, asshole." Karl sat on my chest.

His voice sounded like it was coming from the bottom of a dark well.

He slapped me again. I winced, tried to pull away, but he had a fistful of my shirt. He hauled me up and dropped me in a chair, hovered over me like an avalanche ready to happen. He took the revolver from my holster, took the little automatic from my waistband too.

"Give me my gun," said the Mexican from her cell. "I want to shoot him in the belly."

"Shut your yap, bitch," Karl said. "You're the one fucked all this up in the first place."

"I told you it wasn't my fault," she said. "This cowboy deputy took the keys from Luke Jordan and threw everything off."

Karl went through my pockets, found Jordan's keys. He took his cuffs, slapped one bracelet around my wrist, and cuffed the other to one of the cell bars. "I'll be right back."

The hellcat shook the bars. "Let me out of here."

"Nobody goes anywhere until I get a lid on this. Now shut up and sit tight."

Karl left through the front door. I tugged on the cuffs just for the heck of it, but I knew it was no use. I slumped in the chair. A ragged sigh leaked out of me.

"You are dead, cowboy. You are sitting there dead."

I didn't have anything to say to that. She was probably right.

"You should just have kept your nose out of it," she said. "You had to be a stupid hero cowboy cop."

"Hey, at least I didn't jam a bunch of people into the back of a truck. They could suffocate back there. And it's hot as hell."

"Spoken like a typical stupid *gringo*. The fact that these people are willing to risk death to come to your country should tell you something. The poorest man or woman living in one of your ghettos is far better off than thousands just on the other side of the river. You people know nothing of real poverty."

"I don't have any political answers for you," I said. "Maybe you folks need to work on getting your own country together. That's not my concern. What happens in this town is. What happens to Luke Jordan is my concern."

"In a few minutes, nothing will be your concern anymore."

I jerked on the cuffs again. "Shit."

Karl had left me my Winstons and my Bic. I lit one, tried to puff myself an escape plan.

The hellcat came to the front of her cell. "Give me one of those."

"Go to hell."

She went back to cursing me in Spanish.

Karl came back through the front door. He was so red, I thought cartoon steam might shoot out of his ears. He loomed over me, and I felt the hate vibes radiating off him.

"What the fuck did you do over there?"

"I don't know what you mean."

His backhand spun my head around, little colored lights in front of my eyes. My teeth hummed with the impact. I tasted blood, spit, and it dribbled down my chin. For a split-second I thought he'd broken my jaw. I felt along my back teeth with my tongue.

"I don't want any more bullshit, you little turd." Karl flicked my forehead with a thick finger. "You get me?"

I nodded and massaged my jaw. It would be okay, but it would be sore for a while.

"What happened?" asked the hellcat.

"Billy Banks is lying over there with an axe in his neck. All our cargo is gone."

Cargo. That's what they called human beings.

"Where?" she asked.

"How the hell would I know?" Karl jabbed my chest with a finger. Hard. "You'd better start talking, kid."

Kid. The son of a bitch was only eight years older than I was.

The hellcat shook the bars again, belted out some kind of desperate animal frustration growl. "Will you please open this fucking cell?"

"Just simmer, missy." Karl rubbed his face, blew out an exasperated sigh. "This ain't gonna work, man. It's all fucked up. No way we can hide all this. The town's going to wake up soon and start asking questions and Billy's over there drawing flies. Somebody's going to have to take the fall on this."

The hellcat's eyes narrowed. "You'd better not be looking at me, big man."

"No, you're not believable," Karl said. "Christ, what's Krueger going to do? Where is he anyway?"

"The cowboy," the hellcat said.

"The what?"

"Him," she said. "Pin it on the kid."

That woke me up a little. "What?"

"Hey, that's not bad," Karl said.

"Nobody's going to believe it," I said.

"Sure they will. Hell, we can even pin Luke Jordan on you. Shit, that might just work."

"Why the hell would I kill Luke Jordan?"

Karl bent down until we were eye to eye. "Damn boy, you're just plain dumb, ain't you? Maybe we'll ask Doris, see what she knows about it."

"You can't use Doris to get to me," I said. "She's gone to her sister's."

"That's even better." Karl smirked. "She leaves you, and you take it out on Luke."

"Why the hell would I do that?"

"You just keep pretending you don't know."

"I'll talk," I said. "You try to blame all this on me, and I'll sing like a fucking barbershop quartet."

"You're not going to say jack shit." Karl drew the Glock from his holster. "You were killed trying to escape."

Oh … shit. I felt my sphincter twitch. The bottom dropped out of my gut.

"Shoot him in the belly," the hellcat shouted.

"Shut up," Karl snapped. He pointed the pistol.

I tried to think of something, say anything to make him wait. My mouth was so dry I couldn't make words come out.

"You can't do it like that," the hellcat said.

"I've got this handled, okay."

"Idiot," she said. "You can't shoot him for escaping if he's handcuffed to the cage."

Karl lowered the pistol. "Damn, you're right."

He dipped two fingers into his shirt pocket, came out with a pair of small keys on a ring and tossed them at me. I caught them on reflex. I held them up. The handcuff keys.

"Unlock yourself," Karl said.

"I'm not going to help you kill me."

"You want to die like a man on your feet, or like some squirming coward?"

"I don't want to die at all."

"Tell you what," Karl said. "Sit there and give me shit, and I'll belly shoot you like the *senorita* wants. Do what I tell you, and I'll make it quick and clean."

I stood, pushed the chair away with my foot. A quick death wasn't much comfort, but damn if I would just blink at him like some idiot coon hound and wait to be shot. I'd unlock the cuffs and then make some kind of play, jump at him, try to catch Karl off guard. Anything. I didn't have a prayer, but a one in a million chance was still a chance. I unlocked the cuff on my wrist, braced myself to spring.

"I'm gonna put this shot right between your eyes, kid. I'd say sorry, but frankly I'm just not that sorry." He squinted, sighted down the barrel at my face.

"Drop it, Karl."

Karl froze. The new voice startled me.

"I said drop it."

Karl began to turn his head to look at her.

"Do *not* turn around, Karl. Stay still and put the gun down."

Karl muttered curses under his breath. "You don't know what's going on here, Amanda."

"That's true," Amanda said. "But I'm pretty sure I just heard you describe how you were going to murder Toby here, and that's definitely not in the handbook. Now, put the gun down please." She stood with a two-handed grip on her automatic.

Amanda was athletic and thin, tan, almost as tall as I was. Brownish red hair cut short like a boy's. The khaki deputy's uniform hid sinewy girl muscles, like a tennis pro might have, but I knew she got hers from rock climbing and long distance cycling. I'd seen her score perfect marks on the gun range and armlock truckers twice her size when things got rowdy at Skeeter's.

Karl didn't put the gun down. She kept her Glock on him, and he kept his on me. I stood as still as stone and tried not to piss myself. The hellcat watched from her cell with big brown eyes.

"I'm waiting, Karl." Amanda's pistol never wavered from him.

"Okay, but you put your gun down too, and we can talk about this."

"That's not how it works, and you know it, Karl," she said.

"This is bullshit."

"Karl." Amanda's voice was calm, just above a whisper. "I'm going to give you three seconds to drop the gun.

Three seconds went by and nobody moved.

Bang.

The shot nearly made me crap my pants.

Karl dropped his gun and went to the floor face down, squirming and cursing a blue streak. "You fucking cunt. Oh, fucking shit! You shot me in the ass, you bitch. Damn, that hurts."

"Just stay down, Karl. Toby, get his pistol."

I grabbed it.

"Oh, you complete fucking whore." Karl was making fists and groaning between outbursts, his eyes crushed closed against his ass pain.

Amanda took a step closer, spared me a glance. "I got your message, but when I tried to call, the phone was out. Didn't think I'd be shooting anyone today."

"It's been that kind of night."

She said, "Karl, I'm going to grab one arm and Toby's going to get the other, and we're going to drag you as gently as possible into the cell, okay? Then we'll fetch Doc Gordon. You give us any trouble, and I'll put another one in you. Understand?"

Karl nodded. His face was a sweaty grimace.

We hauled him into the vacant cell, dropped him on the cot and locked it.

"Toby, put that chair over by the far wall and have a seat."

I did what she told me.

She slapped one cuff on my wrist, the other to the radiator.

"Oh, come on."

"I don't have time to hear your story right now, Toby. Sorry. Can't take any chances. We'll see what happens when I get back with the doc."

"Great."

She jerked a thumb over her shoulder at the hellcat. "You can start by explaining who the hell that is."

CHAPTER FOURTEEN

Doc Gordon worked on Karl's ass in the cell. I heard him tell Karl to hold still, but Karl hissed and bitched every time the doc poked at him. Amanda swung a leg over the edge of the desk, regarded me with her hard, cop eyes.

I'd never have eyes like that, I realized. I'd never make it in the cop business because I wouldn't be able to put that expression on my face. I knew Amanda, liked her a whole lot better than I'd liked Karl or Billy. She treated me more or less like a fellow deputy, not a part-time errand boy. But right now she was looking at me like some interesting species of bug under a microscope. She'd been a cop back in Eastern Oklahoma. Claremore, I think. She'd said she'd wanted to live farther out in the wilderness, do outdoorsy stuff like hiking and the rock climbing. So here she was in Coyote Crossing just under a year.

Anyway, I knew I wouldn't be able to lie to those cop eyes. Besides, I needed to tell somebody. Unload. So I started the story at the beginning with losing Luke Jordan's body. She didn't seem surprised to hear about me and Molly, and I figured it didn't really need to be a secret no more anyway since Doris had run off. I told her about the truck full of Mexicans and putting an axe through Billy's neck and my upside down Nova. I told her about Roy's big-rig and the hole I put in the Mona Lisa Motel. I told her about my son.

I felt exhausted by the end, put a cigarette in my mouth.

"You're not supposed to smoke in the stationhouse," Amanda said.

The look on my face must've been the saddest thing in the world because she rolled her eyes and said, "Go ahead then."

I smiled a weak thank you at her and puffed one to life.

"Where's the chief?"

I frowned. "I got a bad feeling he's dead."

"Why do you say that?"

"He went out to the Jordan's place and that was the last anyone heard of him."

"You think the Jordans are part of the smuggling?"

I nodded, puffed.

Doc Gordon came up behind us, cleared his throat for our attention. He wore an undershirt and pajama bottoms and carried a black doctor's back. The pajama bottoms were green and covered with fish. He was in his late fifties and stooped, hair gone completely white. Round, thick glasses. He looked like a man who didn't want to be awake.

"How is he?" Amanda asked.

"I cleaned him up," Gordon said. "And I gave him a shot for pain, so he's sleeping. Bleeding stopped. I got a bandage on him. He'll need to get over to county, so somebody can pry the bullet out, but he'll be fine for a while."

"Thanks, Doc. Send the bill to the town council like usual, okay?"

"Them? They don't get around to paying bills very fast. But there's no hurry, I guess. What happened?"

"Part of an ongoing investigation."

The doc waved that away like he was swatting a fly. "I can take a hint. Fine then. I'll be back in the morning to change his dressing." He left grumbling, but that was just Doc Gordon's way. He wasn't happy if he wasn't grousing about something or other.

I looked at Amanda. "Now what?"

"Now we call in some help. We've got to find the Jordan brothers and the chief, and we've got a crapload of illegal aliens running helter-skelter all over the county." She picked up the phone.

"That won't work."

She put the phone to her ear, frowned. "I thought it was just my phone."

"Nope. I was thinking the main junction box."

"You think something happened to it?"

"Or somebody."

"Damn. This place needs a cell phone tower."

She unlocked the cuffs. "I'm going to level with you, Toby. You're probably going to come out okay with Billy. It was self defense. I don't know what they're going to say about all the other stuff. You can't just let a bunch of illegals loose on a town, and you sure as hell can't crash a truck into a motel. But I need you right now to stay here and watch these two. I'm going to check the juncture box. Stay by the radio, okay? I'm taking the number two squad car." She handed me Karl's Glock. "Just sit tight and stay out of trouble."

"Right."

"Where is the junction box?"

"Across the street from the sewage plant pump house. They clustered all the utilities in one place."

She paused in the doorway, looked at me with her cop eyes one more time. "Stay here."

"I'm not going to do anything more ambitious than smoke this cigarette."

And then she was gone.

I sat there and smoked the cigarette all the way down, then dropped the butt into Billy's mug. The butt hissed out in the cold coffee. Karl snored lightly from his cell.

"Cowboy," the hellcat whispered from her cell. "Talk to me."

I sank in my chair, put my feet up on the desk. "What about?"

"What would it take to get me out of this cell?"

"A stick of dynamite."

"Look at me, cowboy."

I looked.

With thumb and forefinger she tugged the hem of her dress over her knees, showing a taste of thigh. "A girl like me can do special things for you, make you feel like you've never felt before."

"Don't be ridiculous."

"Money, then. I can give you more than you'll make on cop pay in ten years."

"Lady, how about shutting up for a while?"

Surprisingly she did.

I let my chin hit my chest, closed my eyes. I could probably sleep for a week. I felt fatigue pull me slowly into a long, dark drop.

I was on stage in a honky-tonk. I thought I recognized the place, a sawdust-on-the-floor shithole just south of Lubbock. I was playing along with some song I didn't recognize, trying to make the chords, but my fingers couldn't hold the strings down. The strings bit into my fingers, and I jerked my hand away. I wiped the blood on my shirt, saw I was wearing the khaki deputy shirt. I'd wiped blood on the star, and when I tried to wipe it off I just wiped more on.

The drummer yelled "keep playing" at me. I looked at him. The drummer was Billy, blood leaking over his face from the huge gash in his forehead. I tried to climb down from the stage, but the crowd kept pushing me back.

I heard a woman call my name. The voice sounded familiar but fuzzy. I looked around but didn't see her. There was no way to get off the stage. I felt urgently that I needed to get down, the crowd looking at me, the guitar a useless thing in my hands.

"Toby!"

I kept looking for the source of the voice calling to me. "Toby!"

I opened—

—my eyes.

"Toby!" Amanda's voice squawked from the radio.

I shook the cobwebs out and grabbed the microphone. "I'm here."

She said, "Listen, somebody's done a number on this junction box. Looks like they've ripped out half the wires."

"What are you going to do?"

"The state police are an hour away," Amanda said. "I'm going to drive up to the Texaco and put in a call and come right back. Can you hold down the fort until then?"

"No problem. Be careful."

"See you soon. Over and out."

Amanda was being optimistic. The drive from the state police barracks at Morrisonville was an hour, but she'd have to explain what she needed on the phone first. Then they'd hem and haw and get their ducks in a row. Plus Amanda needed to get to a working phone at the Texaco.

I guessed a good two hours. If we were lucky.

After the weird dream, the idea of sleeping suddenly didn't appeal. I took Karl's Glock and my own .38 and the hellcat's automatic and laid them out on the desk, lined them up by size in descending order. I went to the back room and came back with the cleaning kit and went to work on the guns. I started with mine. Karl's was already spotless. The little automatic was such a piece of shit, it wasn't worth cleaning, but I did it anyway.

I reloaded the .38, holstered it.

If I hadn't been so damn tired, the knock on the door might have startled me. As it was, I merely turned toward the front door lazily and squinted, wondering who it might have been this time of night, hoping it wasn't some damn crisis.

Hell, it was the police station after all. Maybe it was even a legit emergency.

"Come in," I called.

Wayne Dobbs stuck his head through the door, took off his hat. He seemed embarrassed to be at the police station.

"Come on in, Wayne. It's okay."

He came in. "I tried to call, but my phone was on the fritz."

"There's a lot of that going around."

"Lightning hit the junction box again?"

"Something. We're looking into it. What can I do for you?"

"I was on my way in to prep for breakfast when I saw some vagrants out by the Tropicana. Thought you might want to know."

The Tropicana was the defunct drive-in theater east of town, about two miles past the Mona Lisa Motel. I couldn't summon up very much civic concern about vagrants.

"I'll make note of it," I told Wayne.

"It's just that there's quite a few of them, and they got a pretty big campfire going. Fire like that could get out of hand."

"What are you doing prepping for breakfast? Didn't you close Skeeter's down last night?"

Wayne frowned. "My morning man crapped out on me."

"Sorry to hear that. More work for you."

"Par for the course. Listen, one more thing. Some of them Jordan boys are tooling around in a pickup truck and they seem pretty pissed off about Luke. I'm not sure what they're going to do. Just thought I'd mention it."

"Did you tell them I was babysitting Luke's body?"

"Sure. I told them what I knew about the whole thing."

Hell.

"Holy cow, that's her right there!" He pointed at the hellcat in the cell. "That's the gal what was talking to Luke right before he got himself shot."

"Wayne, I need you to keep a lid on this."

His face wrinkled up all bewildered. "What do you mean?"

"I mean, we don't need any vigilante stuff."

"Oh, I get you. Sure, mum's the word." He thought about it a moment. "Say, listen, I hope I didn't cause any trouble talking to the Jordans."

"It's okay. Wayne, you seen Chief Krueger?"

"Not since we were all together at closing time. Why?"

"No reason. Just need to check with him on something."

"Well, I best get over to the restaurant," Wayne said. "I got the early shift of truckers and dirt farmers going to want the usual, and if any more of my help craps out on me I don't know what the hell I'm going to do."

"Okay, then. I'll let the chief know about the vagrants."

He flipped me a two-finger salute and was gone.

Maybe when they fired me from being a deputy, I could work for Wayne. He seemed to have trouble keeping help. I guessed the pay probably wasn't so good, but how hard could it be scrambling eggs and flipping pancakes? Or maybe I could work nights and pour beers and such.

Breakfast. The idea of scrambled eggs and a fat slab of ham and a hot cup of coffee made me want to weep. Hashbrowns.

I forgot about breakfast and thought about Luke. The idea that notorious jerkweed and lowlife Luke Jordan just happened to be in the wrong place at the wrong time was just too far out to believe. He was tangled up in this illegal alien smuggling or I was a monkey's uncle.

"Hellcat. Hey, hellcat. You awake?"

"Why do you call me that?" asked the Mexican woman.

"You won't tell me your name."

"No."

"Okay, then. What was Luke Jordan to you?"

"Nothing."

"How was he involved? He had the keys to that truck."

"Leave me alone," she said. "I'm tired."

"Fuck tired. Was he your partner? The Jordans are in on it, ain't they?"

"Go tug on yourself, cowboy."

Shit.

I sighed, stood up and pushed away from the desk. I stuck Karl's Glock in my waistband at the small of my back, shoved the little automatic in the front pocket of my jeans. I walked toward the front door.

"Where do you go?" asked the hellcat.

"Out."

I locked the door behind me and scanned Main Street. Quiet as a grave.

I climbed into Roy's big-rig, tried to crank it up, but it wouldn't start. I guess you could only pound these things so much before they gave out. I popped open the last energy drink and gulped it warm. It almost came right back up. It was just that bad.

The big-rig was shot, and the Nova was belly up. But I still had one set of keys in my pocket, and I couldn't see how it would matter now if I borrowed one more vehicle. I walked down to Luke Jordan's pickup truck. It was still parked where his body should have been.

The inside of Luke's truck smelled like stale beer and armpit. I started it up, and the V-8 rumbled under the hood. The radio wheezed some old country song at me. I let it play. The music seemed to go with the truck.

I'd thought my part of this was all done. I'd been more than satisfied to hold down the fort at the stationhouse and let Amanda run for the cavalry. But I didn't like the idea of the remaining Jordan brothers cruising the streets looking for somebody to fill full of lead, and I had the idea they might stop by the stationhouse sooner or later. Even more than my concern about the Jordan brothers was one last question that kept nagging at me.

I put the truck into gear and headed for Chief Krueger's house.

CHAPTER FIFTEEN

Luke Jordan's Chevy pickup rattled north up the six, past residential streets, the space between houses getting farther and farther apart until I was back into the black of the Okie night.

North of town was not as deserted as the Six south to the Texaco station and the Interstate. Pinpoints of light glittered from ranches and farmhouses here and there. Double-wides on fifty-acre spreads. The soil was better in this direction, some scattered crops, good grass for cattle. My folks' place was about ten miles north of town. Sometimes when I drove by, a pang of loss hit me in the chest, but I didn't drive by that often.

Krueger's place was a few miles out. A nice two-story stone house, garage, empty barn. He didn't want animals. The chief was a solitary man, never married, no kids. I'd been to his house exactly one time, when he had the department and families out for a Fourth of July barbecue. Ribs and potato salad and Coors Light. Chief Krueger was friendly and welcoming off duty. On duty he was all business and hard as a railroad spike.

My first week on duty, the chief took me around on night patrol, showed me the ropes. We passed a couple of rowdies spilling out of Skeeter's near closing time, some college guys on a road tip, Arkansas caps and sweatshirts. Maybe they thought it would be a cool experience for their blog to tie one on in some Podunk whistle-stop. Anyway, the chief give them a warning, friendly but stern, like maybe they should have a few cups of coffee before they got behind the wheel.

The drunkest one got lippy, said he didn't need no fat Okie flatfoot telling him when he'd had enough and started making fat lawman jokes like the chief had come out of *Smokey and the Bandit* or something.

Imagine a volcano about to erupt, the ground vibrating under your feet right before the big explosion.

You wouldn't think a man that big could move so fast. The chief had his nightstick out and slapped across the one punk's knee in one smooth motion. His friend's mouth fell open, not believing, and Krueger poked him a hard one in the gut. The guy bent over, sucking for air. We piled them in back of the squad car, and they spent the night in jail. The next morning, the chief escorted them to the edge of town, and he told them not to come back.

Chief Krueger solved a lot of problems without troubling a judge or the court system. It worked. Coyote Crossing was a peaceful town.

Tonight things had gone wrong.

And if the chief wasn't around to be on top of it, then something bad must have happened. I aimed to find out what I could. I owed him that much.

I turned down the dirt drive, passed the chief's mailbox. About two hundred yards to the house. It was dark, no cars in front, but maybe in the garage. The porch light was dark. I climbed out of Luke's pickup, approached the house slowly. After the night I'd had, it was all too easy to imagine dark figures lurking in the shadows. I didn't want any surprises, squinted all around before climbing the porch steps and knocking on the front door. When nobody answered, I knocked slightly louder. I thought about taking off, but I hadn't come all this way just to knock on the front door.

I tried the knob, but it was locked. I cupped my hands against a front window and looked inside. Not a single light on in the house. I walked around the other side, past a screened side porch to the back. There was a wide patio, table and chairs with a sun umbrella, expensive propane grill set up. This is where we'd had the barbecue. The memory of the ribs made my stomach growl. Potato salad.

The back door was locked too.

I stood there thirty seconds wondering if I was doing the right thing then put my elbow through a pane of glass in the back door, the crash tinkle of shards was way too loud. I reached inside, careful not to cut myself, unlocked the door and let myself into the kitchen. I flipped on the light.

The kitchen looked like something out of the 1950s, old cabinets, ancient gas stove, copper pots and pans hanging over a well-scarred island cutting board. There was a faint smell of disinfectant. No microwave, nothing gleamed new. A coffee percolator sat on the counter near the stove. I only recognized it because my grandmother had one. Somebody needed to get the chief a Mr. Coffee for his birthday. I put my hand on the percolator and the stove. Both cold.

I went through the kitchen and dining room into the living room, flipping on lights as I went. "Chief? You here?" I'd come too far to have the chief blast me with his twelve gauge because he thought I was a burglar. I was ready to throw myself on the floor at any second.

Krueger's house looked like some kind of hunting lodge. Big stone fireplace, deer heads mounted on the wall, dark leather couches, cedar paneling. A dark painting on one wall of mountains and evergreens. It was a bachelor place all right. I walked to the fireplace, looked at the pictures on the mantle but didn't recognize anyone. I stood there a bit scanning the photographs and realized my shins were warm.

I knelt, looked at the fresh ashes in the fireplace. Singed papers in the corner. Somebody had burned something in here recently.

Huh.

I went back into the kitchen, opened the chief's fridge. Nearly empty, but there was a can of Pepsi and I grabbed it, popped it open and drank. The chicken legs I confiscated from Roy's kitchen seemed like something I'd eaten a year ago, but the chief didn't have much, so I closed the fridge and stood there sipping soda.

The chief was something of a neat freak, and if the kitchen hadn't been so damn perfectly clean, I probably wouldn't have noticed the dark spots on his tile floor. I knelt, looked closer without touching. A dark red blotch the size of a silver dollar. Three more dime sized drops leading away into pin-point size drips. The trail led to a door. I pictured the front of the house, the location of the kitchen. The garage. I opened the door to cool darkness.

I felt inside for a light switch but couldn't find it. I fished the Bic lighter out of my pocket and flicked it, followed the feeble glow into the garage. No cars. Dark shapes along the far wall like a workbench and toolboxes. A musty mix of smells, fertilizer and grease.

I walked into something like a spider web and flinched, stepped back and held up the Bic. It was a pull string. I yanked it, and the light came on.

I saw the body first thing, and before my eyes could focus I thought it was Krueger. Somebody had sneaked into the chief's house and killed him. But I saw better a split-second later.

Luke Jordan sat half in and half out of a body bag, slumped in an old brown Lay-Z-Boy patched several places with duct tape. An arm hung down to the floor, the droplet trail caused by blood leaking down one finger. I stepped closer, examined him. The same plastic expression hung on his face. His clothes looked mussed, the pockets of his jeans had been turned out.

Looking into his dead, blank eyes, I didn't have anything much against Luke Jordan at that moment. I couldn't hold a grudge against a stiff. Forget he'd been a total dick in high school. Forget he'd been a rowdy and bully. Forget too many girls thought he was a cool, dangerous stud. Forget all of it. Right then he was just another of the untimely dead.

Something caught my eye on the tool bench. The chief's hat. I picked it up. A red smear of blood along one side. Hell. What had happened to him? I felt something cold crawl up my spine, standing there looking at the chief's blood on his hat like that.

I backed out of the garage, left Jordan and the bloody hat.

I was beginning to think I wasn't going to find the chief. I went upstairs just to cover my bases. In the master bedroom, the drawers were half-open, clothes pulled out. I checked the two other bedrooms. One had been converted into an office, and the chief's desk drawers were open. I took a look. Empty.

I scratched my chin, figuring what it all meant, forming a picture in my head.

And then the lights went out.

I twirled in a panicked circle for two seconds, bumped into a chair.

Okay. Chill.

I felt and fumbled my way into the hall in case it was just the office light that had burnt out. I found the switch, flipped it on and off a half-dozen times. It stayed dark.

I felt my way back to the master bedroom. A bouncing orange light flickered on the windows. I rushed to the window, looked down.

Flames licked up the side of the house.

I ran back to the office, my shin smacking something in the darkness. I grunted, hopped the rest of the way. In the office I saw the orange glow even before I looked out the window. Flames there too.

I ran downstairs as fast as I dared in the pitch black. The living room filled with the hellish, flickering glow from the front windows. I flung open the front door, and the blast of flames knocked me back, singed my eyebrows. The chief's wooden benches and chairs from the front porch had been stacked against the door, the whole pile a raging inferno. I shielded my face with my hands, felt like I was being cooked, eyeballs instantly dry, throat parched.

So much smoke.

I backed up the stairs, closing my eyes against the hot sting. The angry orange glow filled every window.

I rushed into the upstairs bathroom. The window faced the front of the house. I opened it wide, punched out the screen. I looked down, saw the fire hadn't brought down the porch roof yet. If the flames had eaten underneath, I'd fall through and fry. I hoped it was still solid.

I climbed through, caught my foot on the window ledge and tumbled out and down. I hit the porch roof and bounced. I clawed for a grip, tore a nail loose and rolled. The world blurred fiery orange and I was in mid-air, a tsunami of heat washing over me. I hit the ground hard, and the wind *whuffed* out of me. I rolled away from the heat, dust in my face and eyes. I got to my hands and knees, tried to gulp air between fits of coughing. My eyes streamed, nose snotty. The inside of my mouth tasted like hell on Earth.

The house went up fast. I stood on wobbly legs and watched. If I'd hesitated, waited just a little longer to escape …

I stumbled to the barn, found a water spigot. I gulped tepid water a handful at a time, washed my face and the back of my neck. Even this far away from the house, the heat from the fire was almost too uncomfortable to bear. Luke Jordan's Truck was parked too close to the house. Already the hood was turning black from the fire. I wouldn't be able to get near it.

I was stranded again, the walk back to town too long to contemplate.

But maybe I didn't have to go back to town. I wasn't out of it yet. I hobbled back up the chief's driveway toward the Six, trying to massage the bruises out of my ribs. At some point, when this hellish night had ended, I'd need to check with a doctor, make sure nothing important had been knocked beyond repair. Only willpower and stubborn-headed stupidity kept me together.

When I hit the Six, I turned north and started jogging toward the Jordan place.

CHAPTER SIXTEEN

Ten minutes jogging and I had to stop, the stitch in my side like a hot fork in my flesh. I walked, holding my ribs, panting, sweat sticking my shirt to me.

I paused, looked back at the chief's house, the flames visible for miles and miles. I remembered the phones were out. Nobody would be able to call it in. Lucky there were no other houses close. The fire wouldn't spread.

By the time I reached the gate to the Jordans' ranch, I was down to a slow hobble. My body was screaming for me to lie down anywhere, even in the middle of the road, and go to sleep. I pushed the gate, and it creaked open on rusted hinges. I walked the dirt road to the Jordan home. It was a sprawling brick ranch house with a pebble circular driveway in front, untended, scruffy shrubs under the front window, a barn and a few out buildings a hundred yards beyond.

Somewhere a herd of lazy, skinny cows munched dry grass, keeping up the appearance that the Jordans were in the cattle business, and not a bunch of redneck hoods with a finger or two into every disreputable scheme within reach.

It's true that in high school I had disliked Luke Jordan from a distance, but it was the stories of his older brothers, surfacing here and there in excited whispers, that I remembered most as a teenager. The town toughs, bullies and bad eggs. See them coming down the sidewalk, and you crossed the street. And everyone knew they were generally up to no good, yet somehow they always managed to slide, get off on a technicality or maybe a witness would reconsider what he'd actually seen, sitting up there on the witness stand. Only the oldest, Brett, had gone away to the big house. Can't win them all. So Brett was known as the heavy criminal, but it was Jason more than any other brother that made me stay clear of the Jordans.

One thing I'll always remember about Jason:

I was sixteen years old, sitting in my Mom's Aries K car outside the Tastee-Freeze. Tiffany Davies sat in the passenger seat licking a chocolate ice cream cone like she was in love with it, and the only thing I could thing of was how to get her pants down around her ankles. I'd been working her hard, Saturday night dates three weeks in a row, heavy petting and dry humping, and I'd figured that night was going to be go-time. I had a condom in my pocket, pressing a permanent ring in the leather of my wallet.

Jason roared up on a black Harley Davidson, denim jacket, biker's boots, wraparound sunglasses, no helmet, his dishwater hair tied back with a blue bandana. He leapt off the bike and jumped onto the car next to mine, a white El Camino. He stomped across the hood, jumped down on the driver's side, opened the door and pulled Mark Foster out from behind the wheel. Mark was a year ahead of me, skinny in t-shirt, jeans and scuffed Doc Martin's.

Mark didn't get a chance to say anything. Jason had popped him in the nose, a smear of bright blood down Mark's face. It all went downhill from there.

The El Camino's passenger door flew open and Missy Shaw emerged, some Tracy Chapman song spilling out of the car with her. She was in my biology class. I thought she was hot but strange, so I really never talked to her that much.

"Stop it, Jason," she screamed, almost hysterical.

"You shut up," Jason told her.

And she did, shrinking back into the El Camino, eyes so wide with terror.

Jason had Mark back over the hood of the car and just kept beating him in the face.

"Oh, my god, oh, my god!" Tiffany kept bleating next to me.

Jason's girl. Now Mark's girl. Maybe nobody's girl in a second.

Mark had gone all floppy and loose on the hood, Jason still beating down on him. I thought a minute Mark might've been dead. It seemed to take forever for people to erupt from the Tastee-Freeze, five of them grabbing Jason, a couple truckers and farmers and Mr. Iverson in his stained apron.

My mom and dad took me to a safari park one time when I was nine years old. You drove through, stayed in your car, lions and zebras and everything all over the place, and a sign about every two inches reminding patrons to STAY IN YOUR CAR. That's what it felt like sitting there in the Aries K, watching the whole thing through the windshield.

I'll never forget the look on Jason's face, his eyes so calm, yet at the same time blazing some cold fire, a man or an animal about the devil's business.

And that's how I thought of the Jordans now, a whole family of them going about the devil's business. The chief always told me if you start thinking of people bigger than they really are, then you'll never maintain law and order. It's the man with the star on his chest that's big. I tried to remember that as I approached the Jordan household.

A light on in one front window. The rest of the house looked dark. I eased around the back keeping to the shadows. The front porch light didn't cast its glow very far.

The side of the house was cluttered with old engine parts, the rusted hulk of a Pinto, an ancient refrigerator. I maneuvered through the debris, not really sure what I was doing here, hoping answers would present themselves without me having to ask the right questions. I didn't know the questions anymore than I knew the answers. All I knew was everything was wrong and it all started with a dead Luke Jordan, so maybe the Jordans knew the right secrets to make sense of this mess.

So many secrets and so much history for such a small town. Miles and miles and miles of wide open space, yet it seemed like we were in each other's pockets every damn day. Hell, I knew the other side of the coin too. Going from gig to gig, town to town, and every single face was a stranger's. When I was on the road with the band, I felt free, but I often felt lonely too.

I couldn't say which way was worse. I couldn't make my brain think about it.

More junk rose up in my way. I scooted around a defunct dishwasher and an empty, pitted beer keg. A fence with a gate half open leading into the back yard. I slipped through, quiet as I could step.

Just inside the gate, the Doberman leapt for me.

Like some sleek rocket made of solid meat, he flew, trailing slobber, his bark sending a panicked chill straight up my spine. His jaws snapped shut two inches from my face, and he landed in front of me, barking his head off. I backed up where the fence and the side of the house made a corner, petrified. The dog didn't come any closer, and I realized he was on a rope tied to a small tree thirty feet away. There was no way to get around him without coming within range of those teeth. He liked showing me the teeth, his lips curled back in a constant growl.

My hand fell to the revolver, but it never cleared the holster.

"Lucifer, sit!" A new voice from the house.

The dog backed up three steps sat, a low growl still trickling out of it.

An old woman came out of the screen door, little more than a silhouette against the light from inside the house. But I could see the revolver in her hand well enough, an enormous lumpy thing from some old war. She pointed it at me. Compared to the dog, I didn't mind.

"Who's that?"

"Toby Sawyer, ma'am."

She squinted at me, leaned in trying to get a look at me. I could tell she had trouble seeing, but the revolver was so close, I'm sure she'd have no trouble putting one right in my gut.

"You one of Luke's friends? Or Jason's?"

"Not quite, ma'am," I said. "But I was hoping to check with your boys if they were home."

"My grandsons."

Holy shit, Grandma Jordan. When I was eleven, my dad told me she'd shot an Indian. I wondered if it were true. I wondered if that was the same gun. I hoped in twenty years people wouldn't be telling the story about the time Grandma Jordan shot a part-time deputy.

"Are they here, ma'am?"

"No. Come inside."

"Well, if they're not here, I don't want to disturb—"

"I said come inside."

"Okay."

I went through the screen door and found myself in a hot stuffy room, stacks of books, magazines and newspapers surrounding an old overstuffed armchair. The place smelled like fried bologna and Ben Gay.

She motioned with the revolver. "Keep going."

I went through the cluttered room and into a small kitchen. She added a second cup and saucer to a tarnished silver tray, kept the gun on me with the other hand. She added a ceramic pot to the tray. The pot had thin little cracks running up the side, a faded pattern of purple flowers. The cups and saucers matched the pot.

She nodded at the tray. "Bring that please."

I picked it up and followed her back into the stuffy room with all the magazines. She sat in the armchair, motioned at a footstool nearly buried in newspapers. I cleared off the stool and sat, placed the tray on a clear patch of floor between us. I handed her a cup and took the other one.

I sipped. Tepid. A vague hint of mint, slightly bitter aftertaste. She sipped too, her other hand seemingly casual on the gun in her lap. I appraised the old woman, tried to gauge her ability to plug me before I could jump up and run out the door.

Old lady Jordan looked frailer than she sounded, the skin on her face a collection of wrinkled, gray folds. Her gray hair hung long and loose about her shoulders. One eye was completely white with cataracts, but the other eye was bright and vivid blue, seeing everything. Her dress was old and black. Support hose. Ugly shoes. When she smiled, her teeth were so white and perfect they had to be false and gave her a demented Cheshire cat expression.

"I saw Meredith James at Church last Sunday." She said it like I knew who she was talking about, like we were already in the middle of a conversation. "She's recovering from a stroke. She's seventy. You know how old I am?"

"No ma'am."

"Guess."

Why did old people like this game so much? "I wouldn't know, ma'am."

"I said guess."

"Sixty?"

"Don't mess with me, young man. Guess right."

"Seventy-five."

"I'm ninety-six."

"That's amazing." I said.

That must've been the right response because she smiled. "I still cook all my own meals. The boys take good care of me, of course." She sipped tea.

"Where are the boys now, Mrs. Jordan?"

She tilted her head, gave me another long look with her good eye. "You're one of Krueger's?"

"Yes, ma'am."

She *hmphed* like she didn't think too much of that or of the chief. "Looks like you got dragged along ten miles of bad road. You don't smell so fresh either."

"It's been a long night."

"I never sleep at night, haven't for years." She sipped tea, just a little at a time like she enjoyed going through the motions. "When you get my age you either sleep all the time or you never do. I never do. So I'm up all night and hardly ever get any visitors."

"I'm more than happy to sit with you a bit, Mrs. Jordan." I sipped tea to show I meant it. "Can you tell me where Jason and the others got to?"

"You and Krueger need to leave them boys alone. We're good God-fearing white people out here. Every whiskey drinking Indian gets more respect than us, government money, tribal money. Every son of a bitch in the state who can prove a redskin in the woodpile gets a card and all the benefits. Now they're even changing all the names of the high schools so the mascots don't give offense. And my own boys can't do a few extra things to make ends meet without you lot harassing us."

"I know what it's like to be poor, ma'am."

"That's right," she said. "But you and me can't go open no casino, can we?"

"I don't know anything about that. I'm just worried about people getting hurt. It's my job to help look after everybody."

"We look after our own. You want a graham cracker?"

"No thank you, ma'am."

"Wait a minute." With a little effort she stood, waddled to a shelf and brought back a photo album. It was black leather, looked worn and very old. She turned to the first page and set it in my lap before flopping back into the armchair with a little grunt.

I looked at the first photo, black and white, five by seven, thick paper. On the album page below the photo someone had written *Antonia* in thick pencil. A young girl in a *Little House on the Prairie* dress, maybe ten years old, fled across a field of high grass, a slanted log cabin in the background, a slightly blurry windmill beyond that. The sky a flat gray.

The girl looked back over her shoulder as she ran, raw glee on her face, eyes wide as if being chased by a parent or sibling. It was easy to imagine a squeal of laughter, a breezy sunny day.

"That's me," she said.

"Where?"

"Here," she said. "The cabin burnt down in 1937."

"I'm sorry."

"Me and my folks and six brothers and sisters lived in there. Coyotes stole all the chickens the third year. We fought drought and ice storms. My brothers and sisters grew up and scattered, but I stayed. I stuck, by God, and that should be worth something. It should mean something when you endure and stay and the whole world changes around you, changes and forgets you. It should mean something."

"I guess so." But I couldn't say what it might mean. Maybe not anything good.

She sighed, deflated a little into the depths of the armchair. "There was nothing here. The land was raw and the sky was wide and there was nothing. No town. We took the land and made it submit to us. There was nothing, and then there were the Jordans."

It was easy now to understand why the brothers strutted around acting like they were entitled to everything. I could imagine years of this old woman whispering her poison to the boys, making them out to be barons of the endless prairie. Might makes right. Cowboys and Indians. It was hard to think of the Jordans as a family dynasty instead of a mob of rednecks, but the old woman had her own view of the world. Old people always did.

I turned the page in the photo album and the decades flew by. Smaller black and white photos of people I didn't know. A woman on a horse. A gaunt man in an Army uniform, sergeant stripes. A barely recognizable picture of Main Street. Somehow the town looked more prosperous then than it did now.

More pages and more decades. Faded color photos of young boys, shirtless, lined up and mugging for the camera. I recognized Jason Jordan. I looked into his eyes, tried to discern the seeds of evil that would bloom in later years. I wanted to believe it was easy to recognize the bad, that you could see it coming a long way off and have time to duck or hide, like the eerie green clouds that warned of tornado weather. But all I saw was some kid with buck teeth.

When I looked up from the photo album, I saw Antonia Jordan had nodded off, her chin against her chest, snoring lightly, tea cup precarious in her bony fingers. I set the album aside, and carefully took the cup, set it on top of the album. Delicately, I extracted the revolver from her lap and hid it beneath her chair. She'd find it later. Or not.

I tried to see the same evil in the sleeping old woman that I'd tried to see in the old photo of Jason but couldn't do it. Still, I knew it was there, or if not evil then something broken, something that had gone wrong with her as a human being. It's so easy to think of old folks as kindly and cute, but anyone can go wrong. The hardships and disappointments and tragedies of our lives can make us strong or they can twist us wrong and nobody is exempt from this crapshoot. Not old women or Mexican hellcats or part-time deputies.

You spin the wheel and you take your chances.

I stood, felt my knees pop, back sore, ribs still tender. I needed three cold beers and ten hours sleep.

I'd settle for the Jordan brothers.

CHAPTER SEVENTEEN

The room beyond Grandma Jordan's kitchen was a thin unfinished hall, cement floor, exposed wiring, a bare light bulb pumping out sixty watts overhead. A washer and dryer, some paint cans stacked on the other side. I looked at it a minute and thought the room was maybe some kind of buffer zone, a combo laundry storage room between Antonia Jordan's add-on apartment and the main part of the house.

I had no intention of trying to make my way past Lucifer again, so I went through the door ahead of me. I drew my revolver as I went. I didn't want any more Jordans to get the drop on me.

The main part of the house was mostly dark except for a tiny lamp on a roll top desk. It was enough to see, and I took a quick look. The desk was cluttered with mail, much of it going back several months. It seemed like the Jordans preferred to be reminded a few times before they paid bills. Gun accessory catalogs. *Field & Stream Magazine*. Cattle business stuff. Nothing too interesting.

I'd expected the Jordan home to stink as bad as the inside of Luke's truck or strange like Grandma Jordan's add-on rooms, but the house had an inoffensive pine odor which almost masked a faint cigarette smell. I took out a Winston and lit it. A few empty Budweiser cans here and there, ashtrays not too full but not quite clean either. Mismatched furniture. The sofa and most of the chairs were pointed at a giant fifty-inch television. CDs in a half-assed pile by the stereo. Dixie Chicks, Brooks & Dunn, more country stuff. A Def Leppard CD seeming slightly out of place.

The place looked like some kind of redneck fraternity house.

I searched four bedrooms and two bathrooms and a den before ending up in the kitchen. Nobody home, and I didn't see anything that screamed *proof of conspiracy*.

This kitchen was bigger and better than the little thing they'd slapped together for Grandma, but there were dirty dishes in the sink and more empty beer cans on the counter. I opened the refrigerator and eyed one of the several cold Budweisers with lust. Bad idea. A beer might soothe my multiple aches and bruises, but it would probably knock me on my ass too. I searched for an energy drink without luck. A jar of dill pickles caught my eye. I opened it and took two. Crunchy. There was something in a Tupperware bowl that might have been meatloaf, but I decided not to risk it.

Not even cola, nothing with caffeine or sugar. Hell.

I closed the refrigerator and took a glass from the cabinet, filled it in the sink. While I gulped water I noticed something hanging on the wall, a chunk of wood carved in the shape of a key. A row of small metal hooks lined the key for the purpose of hanging car and house keys. All the hooks were empty except for one. I took the key down and had to smile at the key chain.

The words *Harley Davidson* against an American flag.

I left through the kitchen door and found the Jordans' detached garage. I was worried it might be padlocked, but it wasn't and I threw the doors wide. I didn't bother looking for a light switch. The Harley was close enough to the front of the garage to see the chrome gleam in the moonlight. I put up the kickstand and walked it out. Heavy and solid.

The bike looked exactly the same as it did that day Jason pounded Mark Foster at the Tastee-Freeze. I straddled it, a dopey grin spreading across my bruised face. I felt like I could ride this thing to the moon. It felt big. I put the key in and turned. The Harley thundered to life beneath me. I heard Lucifer barking his ass off in the back yard. Screw you, dog.

I gassed it down the driveway and felt like I'd been strapped to a fat rocket. The wind in my hair. I felt like a legend, the big rumble between my legs like I was riding an earthquake. I opened it up wide, tear-assing back south on the Six. I made a promise to myself to get one of these babies.

Thanks, Jason.

I made it back to Coyote Crossing fast and reluctantly slowed the Harley coming down Main Street. I tried to imagine myself back in high school in a cool leather jacket and a pair of shades, all the girls checking out just how fucking cool I looked. I held that thought a second before the grin melted from my face. I wasn't in high school anymore, and there were no girls looking at me.

Still, the wind felt mighty good.

The pickup truck that roared out of the alley from my right missed clipping the motorcycle's back tire by two inches. I flinched, gassed it, hopped the Harley up onto the sidewalk as the pickup swerved back at me and pulled along side. I tried to look over and see who it was, but I suddenly had to dodge a mailbox and a newspaper machine. I wobbled on the bike, swerved back onto the street, ten feet in front of the truck. It came up behind me fast, and I cranked the accelerator and took off.

I glanced at the pickup in the mirror. A black Ford, fairly new. I tried to remember if any of the Jordan brothers had a truck like that, but I didn't think so. I opened up the Harley for all she was worth and put some distance between me and the pickup. I was really flying now and got a little scared. All I had to do was hit a stray speck of dust at this speed, and I'd splatter myself all over the road.

I passed the Mona Lisa Motel and kept going. The speedometer said I was hauling ass at 110 mph. I glanced at the speedometer again to make sure, waited for a cartoon skull and crossbones to roll across.

I slowed a little, killed the lights. I came upon a stand of trees left of the road, a dozen or so scraggly scrub oaks. I pulled into the tall grass, parked behind the trunk of the biggest oak. Five seconds later the pickup flew by and didn't slow. I counted to twenty slowly then got back on the road after them.

A minute later the old drive-in theater came into view. There was a big orange bonfire and about a dozen people milling around. The black pickup pulled in, circled the crowd once slowly then hit the road again and kept going. I wondered how long they'd drive before they gave up and came back.

Then I remembered Wayne telling me about the vagrants and a fire hazard. I rode the bike in slowly to have a look. I got within fifty feet of the people and stopped, put the kickstand down and climbed off. The vagrants were all Mexican, and I even saw my smoking buddy from the firehouse. They all stood to face me, and a couple carried makeshift weapons. The closest was a burly guy with a full beard. He carried a three-foot length of pipe.

I wondered if pulling my revolver would help or make matters worse. I decided to leave it holstered. They were clearly waiting for me to do something. I was waiting for me to do something too, but hell if I knew what.

Then my smoking buddy stepped forward. He had a younger guy in tow, a teenager with a thin pretend moustache and a shaved head. My smoking buddy mumbled Spanish to the kid.

"He says we are out of town," the kid said. "Like you wanted."

I didn't know if the drive-in was officially in town or not, but it was good enough for me. "I'm not here to make trouble. Just be careful with the fire."

The kid translated to smoking buddy who nodded and talked Spanish at the rest of the crowd. The tension seemed to sigh out of them and they went back to the fire, the level of conversation rising again. Smoking buddy motioned for me and the kid to sit with him at one of the half-rotted picnic tables near the concession stand. I nodded and followed along, sat down.

"Tell him I won't bother you people," I said to the kid. "But others will come along sooner or later. You can't stay around here too long."

He translated, and my smoking buddy nodded, scratched his moustache. The talk coming back the other direction lasted a minute.

"We are far away from where we were supposed to be dropped off," the kid said. "We could call someone to come get us. We have a number. Enrique has a cell phone, but it doesn't work."

I shook my head and sighed. "We've never had cell reception around here, and all the phones in town are dead."

The kid translated, and the other guy frowned and talked again.

The kid said, "We worry. The men can walk. We have endured worse hardships." He gestured toward the concession stand. "But there are women and children."

Women and children. Perfect. I stood, dusted myself off and headed for the concession stand, my new pals following. I opened the door, pushed my way inside. A dozen women sat against the wall. More than half held babies or toddlers in their laps. As a group they looked bedraggled, probably dehydrated and hungry.

Hell. What could I do with these people? What could anybody do? They don't teach you this kind of thing at the academy. They threw a lot of civil codes and procedures at me, all in one ear and out the other. But nobody had taught me a damn thing about saving lost souls. You can't arrest starvation or desperation. What these people must've been through, well, I couldn't imagine. And I felt sorry for them, but I also wanted them to go away.

The cramped snack stand stank of sweat and diapers. I moved near the window for a breath of air, wracked my brain what I could do for these people, knowing damn well not a thing.

I leaned on the windowsill, tried to remember what this place was like back when they were showing movies. I loved the smell of popcorn. A chilidog and a Coke. Must've been nice. Mom and Dad had told me they'd brought me when I was two or three, put me in the back seat with a blanket. There would usually be a double feature, something for the kids at first, and then I'd drift off and the second movie would be for the adults. I didn't remember, but I bet it was fun.

I looked up just in time to see the headlights swing into the Drive-in entrance. It was a black pickup truck. Jason's Harley was parked in plain sight, no way they'd miss it.

"Son of a—oh, come on," I muttered.

"Some sort of problem, *señor?*" the kid asked.

"That pickup truck means trouble."

"For us?"

"For me," I said. "Listen. Get out there and tell them

I'm gone. Say some other police car came to pick me up, and I left the motorcycle here. Can you do that?"

"*Si, señor.*"

"Best get everyone out of here." I motioned to the women and children. "Maybe they'll come in for me or maybe not, but it could get ugly." I let my hand rest on the revolver.

He nodded and translated. The kid and my smoking buddy herded the rest from the concession stand. I backed into the shadows, watched through the window. The truck parked three feet from the Harley Davidson. Damn.

One man got out of the driver's side, another from the passenger side. Both held shotguns. Damn. Damn. Damn.

I pulled my revolver, watched and waited.

The guy who'd been in the driver's seat looked only vaguely familiar, a broad-shouldered cowboy with messy brown hair and a square jaw, maybe a couple years older than me. I recognized the passenger immediately.

Blake Harper was a rat-faced string-bean, with hunched shoulders and a bony chest. His greasy hair fell into his eyes and down past the collar of his plaid shirt. Patchy Elvis sideburns. He looked so thin and brittle and bony, I thought one good punch would knock him into a thousand pieces.

Blake had been Luke Jordan's toady little kiss-ass sidekick in high school. Back then, he'd been too cowardly to try anything too ambitious himself, mostly he just stood in the background and laughed at Luke's stupid jokes while Luke pounded some freshman or snapped girls' bra straps. Upon returning home, I'd heard Blake had moved up the food chain half a notch, ripping off cars stranded on the Interstate and stealing mail from people's boxes. All of it rumors and nothing ever proved. Finally, Blake tied a chain to an ATM machine, tied the other end to his pickup and tried to take off. A security camera caught the whole thing, and he ended up serving a couple years.

He got out of prison and returned to Coyote Crossing to resume toadying duties with the Jordans. Apparently, they had the whole roster of douche bags out after my ass.

A group of five Mexicans approached Blake and his pal, including the Mexican holding the length of pipe. Blake lifted his shotgun, and the Mexicans backed off. They traded words, but I couldn't hear. The Mexicans finally moved off toward the bonfire, and I saw Blake and his buddy put their heads together to confer. They pointed, nodded, and Blake's pal headed for the big Drive-in screen.

Blake came straight at me.

I backed up to the service counter, swung myself over, keeping my eyes on the window the whole time, Blake still coming with the shotgun in his hands, not in much of a hurry. I was aware of the doorway to the kitchen behind me, and I was banking there was a back way out.

I let the darkness of the kitchen swallow me as I eased back, stopping when my butt hit something solid, some kind of counter or stove maybe. I kept the door and window in view, still watching Blake's steady progress. He drifted out of sight as he got close, and I braced myself for the front door to open, a tight grip on my revolver.

At first, I thought maybe Blake had changed his mind. I waited, and nothing happened.

Then the door slowly creaked open. Blake wasn't going to blunder in. He was being careful, knew I might be in here. I only wanted him to go away.

The shotgun barrel came in first, then his hand and one of his legs.

I backed around behind the stove, made myself small.

Blake was trying to keep quiet, but his boots scraped against the grit on the floor. He poked the shotgun into every corner, searching. I held my breath. I didn't have any doubt Blake was coming to splatter me with buckshot. Maybe I should jump up quick and shoot first, but I didn't want to. I didn't want to shoot anyone. I just wanted this long night to end. And anyway, Blake's pal was out there someplace with another shotgun and would probably come running. If I shot at Blake and missed, it'd be two against one.

Just go away, you asshole.

He came around the counter, and I heard him poking into cabinets. A second later he was right there, his silhouette in the kitchen doorway, standing there like the perfect target.

And I thought about it. I really did. It would be so easy to point the revolver and squeeze the trigger two or three times.

Blake peered into the darkness, hunched forward trying to see. He reached along the wall, looking for the light switch. When he found it, he flipped it up and down a half-dozen times, but there wasn't any power. He muttered something under his breath I didn't catch and took a step into the kitchen.

I pressed myself back into the dark corner between the wall and the cold steel oven. A trickle of sweat made an itch down the center of my back. More sweat in my eyes. My heart beat like some kind of *whumping* bass drum.

Blake's head turned slowly one way, and then the other.

And then he backed out.

Keep going, man. Walk away.

I heard the front door open and close again. I let out a ragged breath, put a hand on the oven next to me to push myself up, my knees all watery.

I saw the outline of a back door across the kitchen and went for it. I tripped on something and my hand went out. I hit a stack of pots and pans and they clattered and banged on the floor like the end of the world.

"Shit!"

I ran for the back door but didn't make it. The room flashed and thundered, buckshot pellets scorching the pots and pans next to me. Blake stood half in the kitchen doorway, firing blind at the sound. I spun quick, shot twice, and he ducked back.

Blake screamed, "Harris!"

I knew I needed to get out before Harris arrived, but I kept low when Blake swung the shotgun into the kitchen again and blasted buckshot over my head. I fired again just for the noise to make him back off, and tried to work the rusted slide bolt on the back door. I heard him pump another shell and hit the floor again just before he blasted. I shot at his feet, and he backed off again.

"Harris!" Blake screamed. "Goddamn it, I got him trapped in the snack bar. Get your ass over here."

"You're under arrest, Blake." It was worth a try.

"Fuck you, Toby." He stuck the shotgun around the corner and shot the ceiling.

I holstered the revolver and pulled Karl's Glock. I aimed a foot left of the kitchen door where I imagined Blake stood ready to rush in and cut loose on me with the shotgun. I squeezed the trigger four times, chewed up the wall. The smoke hung thick from all the gunfire. I heard a grunt and a thud out in the front area of the concession stand.

I waited a second, kept the automatic aimed at the doorway. I heard a muffled groan. Good. Blake got his. Lie there and bleed, you son of a bitch.

I bashed the slide bolt open with the heel of my hand, and it finally came loose. I kicked the door hard, and it flew wide. I rushed out, the Glock leading the way.

The back of the concession stand: an old dumpster, a rusted junk car. Crappy picnic tables.

The first blast peppered the wall next to me. I dove for the ground. I saw the flash from the second blast. I felt a sting along my left leg and grunted.

Harris.

I looked up to see him breaking the breach on his double-barrel shotgun, thumbing in new shells. I shot at him and the slug *tunked* the dumpster. Harris ducked.

I got to my feet, ran and dove behind the junk car. I raised up just enough to look over the hood. I waited for his head to pop out for a look, so I could blast it off. He stayed put.

"Harris!" I called. "Harris, come out with your hands up. Throw out the gun, and you don't have to end up like Blake."

Maybe that would shake him up.

He didn't say anything and didn't show his face. I wasn't eager to show mine either. I crouch-walked around the other side of the car toward the dumpster. I wondered if I was being as quiet as I hoped. I knew he was crouched on the other side of the dumpster. Hopefully I'd catch him looking in the wrong direction. I tried my best not to step on dry twigs or broken glass or anything else that might make a noise. The distant bonfire and the fading moonlight didn't do a whole lot to help me see where I was putting each step.

I finally nosed around the corner of the dumpster and saw him squatting there, clutching the shotgun and keeping watch toward the rusted out car. I eased toward him, leveled the automatic. One more step, and another. A little closer.

"Don't move, man."

He tensed then said, "Shit."

"I'm going to come get the shotgun. If you move, I'll blast you to hell. You understand?"

"Yeah, I understand," he said.

I moved in slowly, took the shotgun out of his hands and backed away. I flung it behind me out of reach. I didn't have any cuffs and wasn't exactly sure what to do with him. But I did have some questions.

"How many you got out for me tonight? I know the Jordan boys are prowling around someplace."

"Hey, fuck you, Deputy," Harris said. "How 'bout we knock off the chit-chat and you just take me to jail."

"Jail's full," I told him. "Maybe we'll settle things here."

"Bullshit."

Yeah, it was bullshit, but shitbag Harris didn't need to know that. And there was something about a guy squirting buckshot at you that got the heart pumping. If he so much as twitched an eyelash, I Goddamn *would* blow his head off.

"Are you in on smuggling the Mexicans?" I asked. "Or are you just a hired goon for the special occasion of hunting down Deputy Sawyer?"

"You're so stupid. Take me off to the slammer, man. I'm not even going to need my one phone call. I'll be pissing on your grave in an hour."

I raised the pistol to smack Harris in the back of the head when the back door of the concession stand swung open.

Blake stumbled out, one shoulder soaked with blood. He barley held the shotgun with one hand, blasted it straight over our heads, the buckshot not even coming close. It was enough to distract me, and Harris sprang, one hand going to my throat, the other to my pistol. We tumbled to the ground together rolling in the dust, raising a cloud. Each of us kicked and twisted trying to get some kind of advantage.

The gun ended up between us, and we rolled and he ended on top and I pulled the trigger. The Glock barked, and Harris's eyes went wide, his mouth falling open, saliva dripping. He strained to say something, but only managed to heave out this sad croak.

"Here's one for the road," I said.

I squeezed the trigger again, and he convulsed on top of me. His eyes closed, and I pushed him off. I got to my knees and saw Blake stumbling for me. He was trying to swing up the shotgun into his other hand, so he could pump in another shell, but the twelve gauge just dangled from his grip. He finally managed to pump in a shell. I brought up the pistol, and we faced each other. He looked like he could barely stand, might fall over any minute. He'd lost a lot of blood, and his face looked like chalk.

"Drop it, man," I warned. "You're all used up."

A yellow smile spread across his face. "Toby Sawyer, you dumb half-assed musician pinhead bastard. You're small time ... you're nothing. You're walking around dead with a tin star on your chest."

"I'll last longer than you."

He swallowed. "Maybe. Maybe not."

And then the Mexicans were there. I don't know how long they'd been silently moving up to encircle us, but they closed in, made a ring around us, men in front, the dim faces of women beyond. Even in the darkness I could feel them, the thick mass of humanity all bearing down like a single thing with one mind focused on Blake.

He swung the shotgun in a circle, stumbled. Not one of the Mexicans flinched. Didn't even blink. Blake shook the scatter gun at them. "You get back, you wetback fuckers."

"Who you going to shoot, Blake? They'll be on you before you can pump in another one."

"Maybe I'll save the last shot for you," Blake said. "That'd be some satisfaction anyway."

"Big mistake. I can take you into custody, get you patched up. Or you can take your chance with these folks."

"Listen at you," Blake said. "Talking like a for real law man. Well, you can shove your protective custody straight up your ass, you ass ... hole ..." His eyes rolled up, and he toppled forward, his face bouncing off the hard-packed dirt.

We gathered around, watched to see if he'd get back up. He didn't. I thought he might have kicked it, so I knelt, put a hand on his chest, felt a heartbeat. He was breathing.

"Can you guys try to patch him up?" I asked. "Just until I can send somebody back for him. There's probably some towels or something in the concession stand. Just staunch the bleeding if you can."

The kid and Enrique looked at each other, then back at me.

"This man." The kid gestured to Blake. "He try to kill you."

"Yeah."

"Leave him. He will bleed to death. Rats and buzzards need food also. It is justice."

I shook my head. "That would suit me. I'll admit it.

But I can't do it that way. Truth is I think I'd get more satisfaction seeing him hauled back to prison."

They jabbered at each other some more, and the kid said, "We understand. We are not doctors, but we will do what we can."

I knelt next to Blake and took his wallet from his back pocket. He had sixty-two bucks, and I handed it to the kid. "I don't know how far that'll go, but maybe you can feed everyone. I went back into Blake's wallet and found a Visa card. What the hell. I handed it over.

"I don't normally condone this sort of thing, but I suppose Blake owes us."

"We are grateful," the kid said, "but we still have no way to contact our people."

I thought about that a moment then said, "Follow me."

I went back to Jason's motorcycle and hopped on, I motioned for the kid to get behind me. He looked at Enrique who nodded, and the kid got behind me, put his arms around my waist. He kept fidgeting.

"Stay still."

"Sorry."

"I'll take you to a phone, okay? After that, you're on your own."

He told his friends what he was doing, and they all wished him God speed or whatever. I couldn't translate it, but there were a lot of worried looks on brown faces.

I cranked the bike, and we headed back to town.

CHAPTER EIGHTEEN

I parked the Harley Davidson in front of the police station and climbed off.

"Take this bike down Highway Six," I told the kid. "There's a payphone at the Texaco station. They're not on the same grid we are, so it should be okay. You'll need to dump the bike as soon as possible. Anyway, call your people, get out of here soon as you can, because in a while this place is going to be crawling with the law. You understand?"

He nodded and offered his hand. We shook.

"Thank you." He revved the bike and shot away down Main Street. I listened awhile until I couldn't hear the Harley rumble anymore.

I stood there in the last bit of dark. I didn't think I'd ever get used to the sudden quiet. Coyote Crossing could seem like a ghost town in an eye blink. Even in the middle of the day. I'd seen it. Two or three people on the street walk inside, no cars. Not a sound, not even a dog barking. And you could stand there and look in every direction and not see a sign of life nor a hint of movement, like even the breeze had died and gone to hell. That's how it seemed now. Quiet and strange, the thunder of the gunshots and the roar of the motorcycle already fading from my ears. I could almost imagine it had all been a long, bad dream. Quiet.

It didn't last long.

I heard the voices coming down the side street, two of them. They weren't talking so loud, but the voices carried. It's like that at night. Voices will carry a long way, echo off the buildings. I didn't go for my guns. I knew the voices.

Roy and his pal Howard turned on to Main and ambled in my direction. They were having some kind of lazy conversation about fishing and the new resort over to Lake Skiatook and whether or not they'd be able to borrow a boat from somebody Howard knew. I'd heard about the new resort too, but I didn't know anybody with a boat.

The conversation cut off suddenly as Roy passed his Peterbilt parked in front of the station. If I'd been one of those nasty kind of guys, a mean son of a bitch at heart, I'd have started laughing. The look on Roy's face. Like his heart was breaking into little pieces. He stood in front of his battered truck, mouth hanging open, eyes growing bigger by the second. His face convulsed, like maybe he couldn't decide to sob or scream.

"What. The. Hell." Roy stepped forward, put a tentative hand on the hood. Almost like he was feeling for a pulse.

I stepped out of the shadow near the station door. "Sorry, Roy. We had some trouble earlier."

"Some trouble? That's my Goddamn rig! What the hell happened?"

"Settle down, Roy."

He wasn't so drunk anymore and gave me a look like he didn't want some snotty kid with a badge getting all tough cop. I met his gaze, and he took it. He wasn't happy, but he took it. I was the law. Whatever hardass thing he wanted to say, he kept it inside his mouth.

"Don't worry about your rig. We'll get it reported, and your insurance will handle it." I didn't know if that was true, and I sure as hell didn't know what kind of insurance Roy had or if they'd pay a dime. But I said it all like I meant it. And Roy didn't need to know quite yet I was the one behind the wheel of his truck when it plowed through the motel.

"Where you gents going?" I asked.

"We figure Wayne'll open up for breakfast soon," Roy said. "I need something on my stomach." He looked at his truck again. "Jesus."

"Biscuits and gravy." Howard's contribution to the conversation.

"You been home yet?" I didn't figure I could push Roy too far. He might wonder what Molly was doing with my son in his house. I didn't want to have to explain that.

"Not yet," Roy said. "We wanted food first."

"Do me a favor and go back to Howard's after breakfast. I need to make sure Molly feels safe before you go home."

Roy frowned. "It's my house, Sawyer."

"Liability, Roy. I need to cover my ass."

"I don't take your meaning."

"I need her to tell me she doesn't feel threatened. It's routine." Sure.

He shrugged. "Fine. I just want some bacon." He looked at the Peterbilt again. "I can't believe it. I mean … Jesus Christ."

"It'll be okay, Roy."

And I hoped it would be. It was hard to care about Roy's rig with everything that had happened. I'd killed and almost been killed. My life was turning upside down in a single night. But Roy's problems were big to Roy. Everybody's own problems were the biggest.

I watched Roy and Howard waddle toward Skeeter's.

I was out of cigarettes.

CHAPTER NINETEEN

I walked inside the station. It was dark except for the sad, yellow light of the desk lamp. Karl snored in his cell.

"Cowboy," the hellcat whispered. "Hey, cowboy."

"What is it?" I didn't whisper back, but I kept my voice low.

"Your cop lady friend was looking for you. I think you pissed her off. Eh?"

"Well she can come back and arrest me if she wants to." I flopped into the chair behind the desk. "I'll be right here."

"You look like shit," she said. "I mean even worse than before."

"Thanks. I like you too."

"What's holding you together?"

"Cigarettes and energy drinks."

"Some job, eh? You get beat up, wreck your car. They pay you for this?"

"Not very much."

She grabbed two of the cell bars, pulled her face right up against them. "Then get me out of here. Okay? Get me out, and I can get us money. Lots of money, cowboy. More than enough. It goes a long way in Mexico."

"Knock it off."

"Me and you in Cozumel, cowboy," insisted the hellcat. "Don't you know the possibilities? Can't you taste it?"

"Your sales pitch comes off desperate."

"Damn you to hell." She spat at me. It landed way short.

"You wanted to shoot me in the belly an hour ago."

"I don't want to go to prison," she said.

"That's why it's prison."

"Fuck you!" She erupted in a string of Spanish cursing I was glad I didn't understand.

I waited it out. She trailed off and went quiet again. She slid down into a sitting position, rested her head against the bars.

I sat at the desk. The hellcat pouted. Karl snored. It went on like that a few minutes.

Amanda came into the station house, walked straight for me, leaned in, slapping her hand on the desk. She put her nose an inch from mine. "Did you not understand when I said to stay here, you goddamn retard?"

"Take it easy, Amanda." I met her gaze. Yesterday, I would have flinched. Not today. I'd been through too much. Or maybe I was just too tired.

"Don't tell me to take it easy, kid. What did you think you were doing?"

"Somebody had to go look for the chief."

"And did you find him?"

"No. But somebody burned down his house."

That made her pause a second. "What the hell for?"

"Maybe to fry me. I was inside at the time."

"Maybe they thought you were Krueger," she said. "Where do you think he might be?"

I sighed. "Amanda, I think the chief is dead. He'd of checked in or radioed by now."

She nibbled her lower lip, thinking about it. "Maybe."

"And the Jordan brothers are out there right now, looking to do me some bad."

"In that case we'll both stay put this time," she said. "The state police will be here soon, and we'll mop up this mess from there. Jesus, it's turning into a long night."

Tell me about it.

"I'm making some coffee." She headed for the back room where the Mr. Coffee perched on top of the safe.

I didn't know if my stomach could stand any coffee. It was still burbling from the energy drinks. And the station house coffee was this bitter black acid that could melt the paint off the side of a barn. Maybe I needed some food. I wondered if Amanda would let me scoot down to Skeeter's for pancakes and bacon with Roy and Howard. Probably not.

I heard the faucet come on in the back room, water splashing into the coffee pot.

This one time I heard a radio psychologist remark how smells are the strongest triggers for memory, more than the other senses. And I guess that's maybe so. The smell of charcoal reminds me of my father every time, how we'd camp out in the National Park and do hamburgers or whatever. I could be smack in the middle of New York City and smell charcoal and think of a campfire in the woods with my old man. Cough drops made me think of Mother.

But for Doris it was sounds more than smells, I think. I heard Amanda in the back room splashing in the sink, and the sound sent me right back to the trailer. I'd be sleeping in the bedroom, and I could hear Doris through the thin walls making coffee or doing dishes.

I wondered if she was driving straight through to Houston, or if she'd stop someplace, a little roach-ridden motel on the side of the highway. I didn't like the thought of her ragging herself out, driving all night, nodding off at the wheel. I hoped she'd call when she got to her sister's. I did *not* hope she would come back, but I hoped she would call. And anyway, something would have to be done about the boy if I ended up in jail, or even if I had to go off looking for work. She'd need to fetch TJ maybe take him back to her sister's.

Man, I hated the thought of going to Houston every time I wanted to see my son.

Amanda returned and took the chair opposite me. "It's brewing."

"Now what?"

"Now we wait."

"You ever been married?" I asked her.

"No."

"Lucky you."

"I came close once," she said. "We lived together first, and it didn't work out."

"What happened?"

She bit her thumb, shrugged. "We met during this triathlon in Tulsa. You know, run and swim and cycle. We had a lot in common. Sports and outdoor activity. Then when we moved in together things just got all domestic. We hardly did any of that stuff anymore. Just went to work, came home, sat around the apartment waiting to go to work again the next day. I don't know why, but we both knew it wasn't going to work."

"Sounds like you parted amicably."

"Yeah."

The silence stretched.

I said, "I'm going to need you on my side, need you to speak up for me, I mean."

"It'll all get sorted out," she said.

"I killed a fellow deputy." Billy's dead face flashed through my mind. "And we've got another one locked up. I can't lose my son, Amanda. I'm all he's got."

"They'll investigate it. You tell the truth, and you get what you get," she said. "That's all you can do."

"That don't make me feel too much better."

"I didn't say it to make you feel better. I said it because that's how it is. But if you told it to me right, you did everything in either self-defense or the line of duty. At least in the big picture. Some of the details might work against you."

I thought about putting Roy's rig through the Mona Lisa Motel. No, that wasn't quite by the book. Some real professional cop with experience probably would've had it all handled by now, wrapped up neat and pretty. But I was the dumbass, part-time deputy, fumbling his way from frying pan to fire.

Sizzle.

"Anything like this ever happen to you before?" I asked her.

She shook her head. "My career hasn't been so colorful. But I knew a guy who shot a thirteen-year-old kid once. It was dark, and the kid had a toy gun. He was finally cleared, but I don't think the guy was ever the same. Last

I heard he'd gone in with a private security firm."

And least I hadn't killed anyone who hadn't been asking for it. Amanda shrugged. "Anyway, those State boys will be here soon and then we can—"

The cinder block shattered the window, flew through glass and the blinds and landed five feet from us. We both dove to the floor, and I saw Amanda pop back up a second later with her gun drawn. I drew mine too just to feel involved, but I stayed under the desk.

A rough voice from the street yelled, "Get your ass out here, Sawyer, and take your medicine."

The voice sounded like Jason Jordan's, but it could have been one of his brothers. They all had the same rough redneck bark.

"Who is that?" she asked.

"The Jordan Brothers."

"All of them?"

"I don't know," I admitted. "Maybe."

"They want you."

"I'm popular tonight."

"You seem pretty glib about it."

"I'm pretty tired. Being afraid has sort of worn off."

She went up to the window, but stood off to the side in case another cinder block or worse came through. She still had the gun drawn, and I wondered if she was going to lean out and start shooting like in some old western.

"Who's that out there?" she shouted.

Silence. Maybe they thought I was in here alone.

Amanda tried again. "There's a world of hurt heading this way, boys. State Police. If I were you, I'd get home and clear the streets."

I grinned at her. "Why don't you go out there and arrest them?"

"Go to hell, Sawyer."

I laughed.

"You here me out there?" she shouted again. "Clear off."

"We don't have no quarrel with you, Miss Amanda," one of the Jordans yelled back. "Just send Sawyer out."

"You heard him, kid. Get out there." It was her turn to grin at me.

"They're trying to divide us up."

"I know," Amanda said. "They can't afford any live witnesses, and they must know the phones are out."

"They're probably the ones that done it," I said.

"Yeah."

"Send him out," came the shout again. "For what he did to Luke."

"I didn't kill your dipshit brother!" I yelled. Why the fuck did everyone think that?

"Shut up, idiot," Amanda said.

"Well, I didn't do it."

"But now they know for sure you're in here."

Oops.

Amanda shouted, "God damn it, boys, this is a police station and I'm an officer of the law. You've jumped in a lake of shit and you just keep getting deeper and deeper. You get what I'm saying?"

Another pause.

Finally: "This ain't over, Sawyer. Miss Amanda, you get in the way and whatever happens, happens."

I heard an engine rev high, then the squeal of tires, and the engine roar faded down the road.

"Shit." Amanda holstered her pistol and went to the gun cabinet, unlocked it, took out a pump twelve gauge and a box of double-ought. She started thumbing shells into the shotgun. "This time when I say stay and hold the fort I mean it, okay?"

"You can't be going out there."

She kept loading the shotgun.

"The State Police are coming. Just hang in here, and we'll be okay."

"If it were me," Amanda said. "I'd pile a few loads of lumber against the front door and the back too. Couple gallons of gas. That would smoke us out pretty quick. You want to wait for that?"

I didn't think the Jordans were that clever, but then I remembered the chief's house was probably a pile of ashes

206 • The Deputy

by now. Maybe Amanda had a point. Passively sitting and waiting on the defensive had a few drawbacks. And yet I couldn't quite bring myself to believe it was a good idea running out there looking for trouble.

"And anyway, I'm still the law," she said. "I can't let a bunch of rowdies rip up the town. At the very least I have to go keep an eye on them."

"I still don't think it's a good idea."

"I didn't ask your opinion." She went to the gun locker, came back with another twelve gauge and set it on the desk in front of me. "Hold the fort."

She opened the front door, paused before stepping out, looking up and down Main Street. She gave me one last look, walked out and closed the door behind her. I went and locked it. A second later I heard her squad car crank and drive away.

"You're all alone now, cowboy," came a soft voice from the cell.

"I still have you, hellcat."

"You know those men will come back," she said. "And if they can get inside, then they will kill you."

"Maybe."

"Fool. Let me out, and we will escape."

I tried to imagine it. Not seriously, just for something to do. I imagined her in a bikini or maybe topless on some Mexican beach. I sipped on some kind of rum thing with an umbrella poking out the top. There's a reason they call them fantasies. Because it's not life. I had to stay in my life and take care of my son. And anyway, how long would something like that last before the money ran out or she stabbed me in the back? But in my fantasies, she looked pretty good naked, the surf splashing up around us.

"What are you thinking, cowboy?"

"Nothing. I'm not thinking a thing."

I sat at the desk and put shells in the shotgun.

CHAPTER TWENTY

Amanda had left before the coffee was ready. I filled a Styrofoam cup and caffeinated myself in her honor. The coffee didn't do much for me, but I drank it anyway. I swallowed and winced.

Like battery acid.

At some point I was going to hit the wall. A man can't go forever on adrenaline and caffeine. I wondered what it would look like. If I'd be walking or in mid-sentence and then suddenly my eyes would roll up and I'd collapse into a snoring heap, slip into some kind of turbo coma. Or if my head would just explode and splatter brains all over the room.

I heard the engines outside so soon after Amanda had gone, it made me wonder if they'd been watching and waiting for her to leave.

The revolver hung heavy and reloaded on my hip. I grabbed the shotgun, flipped off the desk lamp. I stood in the darkness, palms sweating on the twelve gauge, strained to listen. A pale green light flickered from the obsolete computer in the corner. Another sad glow from the radio dial. Just enough light in the room to keep from bumping into the furniture.

"They are coming for you, cowboy." The hellcat's whisper was so low, I thought maybe it was a voice in my head.

The engines cut out, and I heard car doors *thunk* shut. I took a step forward, tried to catch a hint of movement through the wrecked blinds that still hung over the shattered front window. I could not make my breathing quiet down, breaths coming shallow through my mouth, my heart thumping up to speed.

I swallowed hard and waited.

Would they bust in all of a sudden with gun blazing, or would they burn me out like Amanda said? If they had the balls to torch the chief's house then why not the station? Sure. Or maybe they'd come at me from two directions at once. I glanced over my shoulder at the door to the back room, thought about the other door out to the alley. Had I locked it? I couldn't remember.

Hell.

I went to the back room, trying to stay quiet. The room smelled like gun oil and bitter coffee. My mouth tasted like acid. I reached for the knob to check the lock. And froze.

The knob was already turning, so damn slowly so as not to make any noise, I guess, but there was still this slight rattle, and I'd never have heard it if I hadn't been standing a foot away. And maybe if I'd been thinking clearly instead of feeling my gut flip-flop and my heart beat in my throat, I would have thought to put my shoulder against the door and hit the lock.

But I stood there watching the doorknob turn like some dumbass in a cheap horror movie.

And then someone was pushing it open. Somebody was coming in.

I held my breath and stepped behind the door, pulling the shotgun in close to my chest. The door opened inward until it was an inch from my face. Let him come in. Let him go by. Take him from behind. Sure. It seemed pretty simple when I rehearsed it in my head. So how come my legs felt like noodles? *Stay focused, idiot.*

He was trying to be quiet and not doing a bad job, but the old floor creaked with his footsteps, one after the other pretty slow as he eased his way in. I saw his fist first, wrapped around a short-barreled revolver, then his arm and then the rest as he went through toward the main part of the station house. From behind it could have been Jason, or maybe it was one of the others. Too dark to be sure, and anyway the brothers were all built more or less the same, this one maybe a bit on the larger side.

I waited two more seconds in case another brother came in behind him. I didn't want to get caught in the middle. When I was sure I was only dealing with one, I stepped out and leveled the shotgun at him. Just shoot, I told myself. Pull the trigger.

No, do it proper.

"Drop the gun." I said it pretty quiet, but I tried to sound mean.

His shoulders hunched and he froze. "Damn it."

"Put the gun down. I mean it."

He dropped it.

I thought how cool and threatening it might sound to pump a new shell into the chamber, but that would only eject a good one. "Now I want you to turn around nice and slow, and—"

He spun fast, grabbed the shotgun barrel and pushed it out of the way. If I'd fired the blast would have gone past him, but I didn't even think of pulling the trigger. I was too surprised. The shotgun flew away. I stepped back, mouth falling open, probably to say something clever like *hey, stop that, no fair.* But I never got any words out.

He stepped in, fist coming up hard to pop me one in the mouth, mashing my lips against my teeth. A little bell went off inside my skull. I tasted blood, took another hit on the jaw, tumbling back along the lockers before I figured it was time to give a little back.

I put my head down and pushed forward, gut punching him. My fists didn't seem to bother him, and he brought a knee up into my groin.

Little multi-colored firework explosions went off in front of my eyes, and all the air went out of me. I shuffled backwards as fast as I could, trying to put a few feet between us and catch my breath. Except I couldn't catch any breath. When I tried, my throat made a deep hoarse sound.

He wasn't about to let up, came at me fast. I reached out for anything to hit him with, and my hand landed on the handle of the coffee pot. I splashed it straight at him, and the hot coffee caught him full in the face.

He screamed, hand going up to claw at his scorched eyeballs. I broke the coffee pot over his head, and he staggered and cursed. I hit the side of his face with my fist, mustered everything I had and hit him again. He went down and didn't get up.

I slumped against the wall, gulping for air. The ache spreading out from my groin almost made me puke. I thought also I might have wanted to cry a little bit, but I didn't. I gave myself thirty seconds to rest, then I pushed myself up and hit the light switch.

It wasn't Jason on the floor but Matthew. A little bigger and slower and dumber than Jason, younger than all the rest except for Luke. I took a spare pair of cuffs from my locker, slapped one bracelet on Matthew's wrist and the other to one of the locker handles. I picked up the shotgun and limped back to the front part of the station house, just in time to hear all hell breaking loose on the front door.

They must have been using something as a battering ram, because each slam almost banged the door off its hinges. On the fourth bang the door popped open and bodies filled the doorway, wide-shouldered silhouettes all holding rifles.

I lifted the shotgun and fired.

The whole station house filled with the thunder. The hellcat screamed, and the lead man in the doorway convulsed and pitched forward. Some guy I'd never seen before, another Jordan toady, I guessed. I pumped in another shell and fired, but the others had already retreated.

A hand came around the corner and filled the station-house with random pistol fire. I ran forward and threw myself behind the desk. Bullets *pinged* around the room. Pencils and paper on the desktop danced and flew in all directions. I raised up, eyes and shotgun just above the edge of the desk, ready to blast anyone who came through. I didn't plan on arresting anyone. Shoot to kill.

There was a lull in the gunplay, and I heard quick footsteps and muffled voices.

A bright, flickering orange blur flew threw the doorway in a low arc, landed with the sound of broken glass. The gasoline spread and a wall of flame sprang up as if by magic, washing the stationhouse in hellish dancing light, The wave of heat hit me, and I hoped there wasn't another Molotov cocktail following the first or things would get impossible pretty damn quick.

I leaned the shotgun against the desk and grabbed the key ring, ran to the hellcat's cell and unlocked it, swung open the door.

"Quickly, out the back!" She made to run past me.

I grabbed her wrist and hauled her back, drew the revolver with my other hand but didn't point it at her.

"Are you insane," She said. "The fire will spread."

"Get that fire extinguisher off the wall over there." I pointed with the revolver. "I'll cover you."

"If we run, we can make it."

I put the gun in her face. "Get the Goddamn fire extinguisher!"

Her eyes stabbed hatred at me, but she bit off whatever curse she'd been about to offer and ran to pull down the extinguisher. There was a pin she had to pull and a handle to squeeze. She started messing with it, and for as second I thought I'd have to put down the revolver to show her how. But she got it right and pointed it at the flames and squeezed the handle, a blizzard of white whooshing out, shrinking the fire a bit at a time.

And I guess that's what they'd been waiting for because then suddenly Clay Jordan filled the doorway with a deer rifle in has hands and brought it up to his shoulder for a shot.

I squeezed the revolver's trigger three times. The first two shots chewed up chunks of door frame, splinters of wood flying around Clay's head. On the third shot, Clay dropped the deer rifle and grabbed the fleshy part of his upper thigh. He threw his head back and yelled. I saw hands yank him back from the doorway.

The hellcat had half the fire out and seemed to have the jump on the rest. Maybe if—

Blinding pain erupted at the base of my skull. I staggered forward, but somehow kept my feet, turned around, trying to bring the revolver to bear, but it felt like it weighed a ton. I saw a long, flat piece of metal swing down and smack my hand open. The revolver flew away.

I saw now that it was Matthew Jordan hulking over me. In the firelight I could see one ear bloody from the bash I'd given him with the coffee pot. He was still handcuffed to the locker door which he'd ripped off the hinges and was using as a club. He cranked it back for a swing at my head.

And got a face full of extinguisher foam. The hellcat was there, thrusting the extinguisher nozzle at Matthew and running out the rest of the foam.

He coughed, pawed at his eyes. "Fucking bitch."

"I owe you this, Matthew." I kicked him in the balls. Hard.

He let out this little squeak and went to his knees. One hand still wiped at his eyes. The other went to his groin. His face went so red I thought he might rupture.

I picked up my revolver and slapped him in the side of the head with it. He flopped over like a dead fish. I lifted the gun to bash him again but stopped myself. I wanted to, but no.

I motioned to the hellcat. "Help me lift him. We can drag him into the cell and—"

She slammed the empty fire extinguisher into my gut. I bent double sucking for air and went down, looked up just in time to see her vanishing through the back room.

I lurched to my feet, took three steps after her and stopped. Forget it. The one that got away. She was a criminal, probably a killer. The hellcat had trafficked in human lives across the border. The star on my shirt meant I was supposed to go get her, lock her up. But she'd helped me in the instant I'd needed it, right when Matthew Jordan was about to smash my head in. That probably didn't go very far to balance out whatever wrongs she'd done, but it would have to do for now.

And anyway I had bigger worries. More Jordan brothers who wanted to kill me. And the station house was still a little bit on fire.

I grabbed a blanket from the cell, used it to smother the last few patches of flaming floor. That put us back mostly into darkness, except for the extra street light coming through the open front door. I dragged Matthew into the vacant cell and clanked the door shut.

It was suddenly weird and quiet in the stationhouse. I couldn't even hear Karl's snoring anymore, and I wondered how he could have kept sleeping with all the gunfire and mayhem. Maybe he was pretending.

Let him pretend.

I drew the revolver and took a few steps toward the front door, cocked an ear and strained to listen. For a second I thought—hoped—the rest of the Jordans had pissed off. Maybe shooting Clay in the leg had stung them into giving up. But I could still hear them out there, voices raised like maybe they were arguing.

Maybe deciding what they were going to do about me. Maybe toss in another gasoline bomb.

No more waiting. I grabbed the shotgun, loaded fresh shells. Time to take it on the offensive.

Showdown.

CHAPTER TWENTY-ONE

I had to do it fast.

Any other way and I'd lose my nerve or just collapse from exhaustion. There wasn't much left in me, but I wasn't going to fold, not yet. This would finish it. I had to make it to the end. So I took a deep breath, dug down deep for that last burst of adrenaline, pushed away every ache and pain that throbbed along the length of my entire body.

Time to kill some guys.

I went through the backdoor and into the alley, pumped a shell into the chamber. I circled all the way around the firehouse at a slow jog, hit Main Street and turned back toward the station. I kept close to the buildings, jogging in the shadows.

I could see them up ahead, two pickup trucks, one facing in each direction, blocking Main Street, headlights on. I saw Jason and Evan standing to either side of the stationhouse door. They both held deer rifles and looked poised to charge in at me. But I wasn't in there.

I was out here.

And bringing it strong.

I ran at them fast, lifting the shotgun. I got pretty close before Clay saw me. He sat in the back of the closest pickup, foot propped up on an Igloo cooler, white bandages around his wounded leg, a red blotch seeping through. He turned his head and saw me, his eyes going big as hubcaps as I sprinted forward. Home stretch. I ran as fast as I could make myself while still keeping the shotgun up.

Clay overreached for the deer rifle in the bed of the truck and fell off his perch, rolled out of the truck and hit the street with a grunt. He stood, hopped on one foot and reached for the rifle again.

I cut loose with the twelve gauge.

The shotgun bucked in my hands, buckshot splattering across Clay's torso. He convulsed like he'd been hit with a million volts, shrank to the ground and sat in a bulky pile of dead.

Jason and Evan spotted me. And I looked at them and our eyes met and just like that it was on, as if the eye contact had triggered some primal, animal charge.

I started running again, pumping in shells and firing and pumping. I was a screaming, running blizzard of buckshot, spitting fire. Thunder rattling the whole town. They ran at me too. Both crazy with banshee yells. We were a hell of a collision in the making.

I had the advantage, spraying buckshot. They ran awkward, shooting, trying to work the bolt actions on the deer rifles. Try it sometime, shooting and running at the same time. The shots went wide, and I almost didn't care if I hit anything or not. I wanted noise and death. Let it all finish here. Pump, shoot, pump.

Twenty feet apart I made Evan's face disappear in a horrible spray of blood and flesh. I pumped, swung the shotgun at Jason. Everything slowed. He worked the bolt action, eyes like a frightened rabbit's. I could see all the mistakes in his face. He knew. The fear bringing it home. He knew in that moment it had all been a mistake, that he was going to die bloody and bad.

But he kept trying. I'll give him that. He was game. He worked the bolt, tried to bring the rifle level for a final shot. Maybe he could get lucky. I shot from the hip, and blood exploded across Jason's chest. The deer rifle flew away. He fell backward, slowly, like he was falling through cotton. That's how I saw it. He hit the pavement and bounced. Lay there with his eyes wide open.

I thought he was dead, but he suddenly violently sucked for air. He coughed and gasped.

I knelt next to him, didn't even feel angry. Didn't feel anything.

Jason's eyes focused on me. "You."

"Me."

"You ... fucking ... fuck." His breath came shallow, blood on his lips. I could almost hear the wrecked machinery of his guts and chest grinding out his final seconds.

"Why do you think I killed Luke, Jason?"

"We all know it was ... you ... son of a—" He broke off in a fit of coughing, spasms along his whole body.

"Why?"

"Call an ... ambulance."

I grabbed two fistfuls of Jason's shirt, lifted his head off the road. "Why did I kill Luke? You got me pegged for it, don't you? Okay then, tell me why."

"Don't be s-stupid." Jason coughed again, more blood foaming out of his mouth, running down his chin, face going so white.

I shook him hard, his eyes pin-balling in his skull. "I asked you a question, Jason."

"You know why," he said. "Luke and D-Doris. Jealous, so you ... killed ..."

He froze, like somebody hit the pause button on his face. And suddenly he seemed plastic, his eyes like glass. I checked for a pulse. Nothing. I set him back on the ground and sighed over him. He looked smaller somehow, like he'd shrunk there on the road when the life had gone out of him.

I looked at his face. I wanted to see that Jordan sneer. I wanted to see the wild eyed rage I'd seen so long ago when he'd beat the hell out of that Mark kid at the Tastee-Freeze.

That was the Jason Jordan I'd hoped to kill, the animal, the reckless bully. The Jason that deserved to be gunned down in the street.

But all I saw was fear. The last expression on Jason Jordan's face, his gaze fixed into the distance, frozen stare at the big unknown coming right at him. I didn't even want the answers to my questions anymore. I'd had bad answers to too many questions already. There was nothing left to do but haul away the bodies and hose the blood off the road.

People were coming out to the street, wrapping themselves in bathrobes, putting on glasses. I don't know why, but I felt embarrassed to have them looking at me. But I supposed I'd have been curious too.

"Back inside, folks," I yelled. "Everything's under control." I stood, made some kind of everything-is-okay gesture, hoping they'd all scoot back inside without question.

"What are you playing at, Toby?" It was Richard Macon, the hardware store owner. "Where's the chief?"

"The chief's on his way," I told them. "By order of the Coyote Crossing Police Department, I'm asking you to all go back inside."

"I've known you since you were six years old, Toby Sawyer," Macon said. "Now, tell me what in blue blazes is going on."

"You know me, and I know you too, Mr. Macon." I thumbed the tin star on my shirt. "But tonight, I'm the law. Now you people get your goddamned asses back inside."

And they did.

They grumbled and gawked at the bodies in the street, but they went. Soon doors were closing. I saw only a few faces peeking though curtains. Maybe I had some kind of authority they believed in, or maybe the fact I'd lied about the chief being on his way was good enough. Or maybe when a man with a gun tells you to do something, you do it.

I picked up the shotgun and put it on my shoulder, sucked in a big lungful of night air. Night. There wasn't much left of it. The sun would be poking up over the horizon soon. The night was over. Everything was over. No more Jordans. No more Mexican smugglers. With morning would come the fallout. The State Police with mops and brooms and hard questions that I didn't have all the answers for.

Hell.

I could use a bed. Maybe a hundred hours sleep.

I went back into the station and tried the phone, but no luck. The whole place still smelled scorched. It was a hell of a mess.

"Goddamn, son, what the hell did you do to this place?"

I flinched at the sudden voice behind me, turned and saw him coming from the back room.

"Been one hell of a night, ain't it, boy?" said Chief Krueger. "I suppose you might have a few questions."

CHAPTER TWENTY-TWO

I didn't have jack shit when I came back to Coyote Crossing. Nothing but a dilapidated trailer and a headstone with my mother underneath. Frank Krueger had been like some salty, distant uncle. The chief had known my father, not a lot but some. I told him I'd somehow managed to squeak through the academy and he tossed a part-time job my way, something to keep me in beer and cigarettes until I moved on. He put his trust in me right away, and that gave me a little pride when I didn't have much else to cling to.

But I didn't move on. That had been the plan, but it just didn't happen. I'd stayed. Krueger must have felt like he'd been stuck with some idiot relation, but he never said a word. Never treated me like a charity case. Yeah, I'd pulled grunt work and crap night duty. But the chief never acted like he was tossing scraps to a mutt. Which was more the truth.

Things seemed to have changed since he was standing there pointing a pistol at me.

I shook my head, tried to clear the cobwebs. So tired. "Chief?"

The chief *tsked*, shook his head too but more like in a sad way, like he had to put down a pony with a broken leg. "You just couldn't go home and mind your business, could you, son?"

Shit.

"Did you really gun down all them Jordans?" He chuckled. "Jesus, boy. I got to hand it to you. I didn't think you had it in you."

I looked him over then said, "You're not wearing your hat."

"Huh?" He ran his hands through his thinning salt and pepper hair. "Oh, yeah." He grinned. "It got smudged."

"I thought the blood … It wasn't yours."

"Nope," Krueger said. "I got my hands dirty and got it on my lid. I guess maybe you got the wrong idea."

"You burned down your own house, didn't you?"

"I want them looking through the rubble for my body," he said. "Give me a little more time to get away, find a place to lay low."

I felt something like lead grow cold and heavy in my gut. "So you were in it with the Jordans and the Mexicans the whole time."

"Hell no," Krueger said. "I'd as soon have a pack of chimps working for me as the Jordans. Just Luke. We paid him to drive sometimes and to keep his mouth shut. Dumb son of a bitch can usually scrape enough brains together to take his pay and go on about his business without causing any trouble."

"But not tonight."

"No, not tonight," Kruger said and sighed. "Horny bastard had to play funny with the sister of one of those banditos. Shouldn't be surprised. Luke never could keep himself zipped up. But I guess you already know all about that."

I summoned everything I had into a cold stare. "I don't know what you mean."

He smiled sadly, shook his head, and just for a minute the colorful old uncle was back. "No, I guess not. That's fine. But anyway Luke Jordan got himself dead."

"With the keys to the truck in his pocket," I said.

"I got back to Luke with a body bag, wrapped him all up like it was police business. Didn't want an audience while I searched him. People were looking out their windows. And I didn't want the keys locked up in the evidence closet. So I took him back to my place. Luke was supposed to give the keys to Billy before he went off drinking at Skeeter's." For just a second, the chief looked pained. "I found Billy's body. You did quite a number on him."

"He needed it."

"I can understand that," Krueger said. "Just a damn shame is all. The whole situation's just a damn shame, and that's for sure. If things had turned out just a little different … well, they didn't, and here we are. A shame."

"What's the shame, Chief? That Billy's dead, or that you can't smuggle illegals no more?"

"Now you just come down from your high horse, Toby. I care about my people. I care what happens to Billy. I'd care if it was you too. Fact is the smuggling was about to dry up anyway. This Mexican crime gang brings them over the border, and they come through here and get spread all over. Some to work mines out west or other places to work the crops. This was a quiet little nowhere stop to switch drivers and get the wetbacks some food and water. But there's federal people sniffing around up north and border patrol getting tighter down south. Too risky now. Too bad we didn't shut down a little sooner. Could have saved some trouble."

Some trouble. I understood now how Roy reacted when he'd seen his truck all banged up, and I'd said there'd been some trouble. Understatement of the fucking year.

I nodded at the gun in his hand. "So what happens now?"

"Looks like I got to get the hell out of Dodge," Krueger said. "No way to cover up this mess. You've had a busy night. But I don't blame you. I surely don't." He shrugged. "Shit happens, as the saying goes. No grudges."

"No grudges. That sounds good. So maybe put the gun away."

"No, sorry, son, but I can't do that. I'm going to shoot you all right, but it's purely practical, not cause I'm upset with you. I promise. There's just no other way this can happen."

My heart sank all the way down to the bottom, but I couldn't help thinking at least it would be over. The long hard night would end at last. Maybe somebody would call Doris and tell her to come get the boy. Thinking of my son brought that ache behind my eyes like when I'm about to start crying.

Oh God.

"Sorry, son." And Krueger really did look sorry. Sorry, old and tired. "But I got to think of myself now, and this is the simplest way."

He raised the pistol, and I felt a warm, fat tear roll down my cheek.

"Stop right there, Chief."

Amanda had come through the back, had her pistol aimed at the chief, walking slowly forward. I could have kissed her.

Amanda said, "I'm making a habit out of saving you, Toby. Maybe you'd better—"

The chief didn't hesitate, spun fast, bringing the pistol around. Amanda fired. The pistol flew from Krueger's hand. He grunted, clenched his teeth, and brought the bloody hand to his chest. His face went pale, sweat breaking out on his forehead. His breathing went fast and heavy like he'd just run a mile.

"That's some shot," Krueger said. It was an effort for him to talk. Blood spilled down his wounded hand. "Just like Wyatt Earp."

"I was aiming for your chest," Amanda said.

Krueger chuckled.

She spared me a glance. "You okay, Toby?"

I nodded. "But it was close."

She edged around Kruger toward me, keeping her gun on him. She backed up against the cell, fished into her pocket for the cell keys. "We'll put him in here, and then call the doc to come—"

One arm came through the bars of the cell and went around Amanda's throat. Another arm grabbed her gun wrist, pointed the pistol at the ceiling. She struggled, but the thick arms held her tight against the bars. Amanda went purple, her slim hand pulling uselessly at Karl's massive forearm.

I turned, made ready to leap for my revolver on the floor.

Even wounded, the chief was too quick.

He was already coming up from the floor where he'd knelt to pull a small revolver from an ankle holster, probably the .32 I'd seen him cleaning once in awhile when things were slow around the station. Not a powerful gun, but plenty enough to make me pure dead.

I watched as Amanda kicked and twitched and then went limp. Karl released her and she slid to the floor.

"She dead?" Krueger asked.

"No," Karl told him. "I put a sleeper on her." Karl limped in his cell, held himself up by the bars.

"Can you walk?"

"No way," Karl said. "Bitch shot me. I'm stiff all up and down one side. Couldn't take more that two steps."

"That's a damn shame."

The .32 spat fire twice, and Karl's eyes went wide as he fell back on his cot, bounced off and hit the cell floor.

"Why in the hell did you do that?" I asked.

"I need a pair of good legs, and Karl would have wanted his cut of the money."

"You could have given it to him."

"And I would have too if everything hadn't got so messed up," Krueger said. "But the situation has changed. I'm going to need every dime if I have to go on the run. I might try to get to Mexico. Hey, that's probably some kind of irony or something. All this time I been bringing wet-backs north. Now I got to smuggle myself south."

He looked at the bodies on the floor and sighed. I sighed too. In such a short span of time the station had been torched and wrecked, bodies littering the floor. Surreal. One of Molly's words.

"Okay," Krueger said. "Best get this show on the road." He waved toward the back room with the revolver. "Let's go."

"What do you want from me?"

"I told you I need a good pair of legs." He held up his bloody hand. "And two good arms. I need you to carry something to the car for me."

"And then you'll shoot me? Fuck that."

"Okay, I won't shoot you," he said. "You help me, and I'll lock you in the cell. That'll give me a head start."

"And I'm supposed to trust you?"

"I could shoot you now and end all the suspense, make do best I can with one arm."

I headed for the back room, and he fell in behind me.

"Okay," he said. "Go to the safe. I'll tell you the numbers, and you work it."

He told me the numbers and I spun the dial.

"Open it."

I opened it.

I didn't think I had enough energy left to be surprised by anything. I was wrong. The safe was packed top to bottom and front to back with tight bundles of cash. It was hard not to be impressed. I could slave all my life and probably never see so much cash.

"In the last locker there's a gym bag," he told me. "Fill it up."

The bag was cheap, bright red and said *Razorback Pride* on the side with the Arkansas pig logo. I unzipped it and started loading the cash. None of the bills were new. Wrinkled. Various denominations, fives, tens, twenties. The variation made it hard to guess the total amount. A lot. I stuffed in the last bundle, zipped up the bag. The cash barely fit, the bag bulging.

"Good," Krueger said. "Now go back to the same locker and get that accordion file folder. Lots of names and embarrassing facts in there. I'll probably burn most of it, but I need to go through it all first."

I went back into the locker, got the file folder.

"Now grab it all up and let's go back out to the alley. I'm parked back there."

I went out ahead of him, feeling like there was a big bullseye target on my back. I'd expected to see his cruiser, but it was his personal car, a big luxury Chrysler about a year old. The chief wasn't a pickup truck kind of guy.

"Stand over on the other side of the car."

I did.

He dipped his hand down to his pocket, still holding the revolver, and hooked his keychain out with his little finger. It was awkward going, but he wasn't about to drop the gun, and he couldn't use the other hand.

He pulled the keys out and flung them at me. They bounced off my chest and hit the ground. I set down the bag of money and the file folder, bent and picked up the keys.

"Open the trunk," Krueger said. "Load it up."

I opened the trunk, picked up the files and money. I felt like I was moving through mud, my arms and legs like cold stone. These were the last moments of my life. Lifting the cash, loading the files, closing the trunk. My last actions on earth. I felt I could hardly breath, like life would leave me all on its own before the chief could even pull the trigger. Part of my brain told me to jump him or run for it or anything. But I didn't do it, couldn't make myself do anything but obey.

When the trunk *thunked* shut, it sounded like a cold metal coffin closing.

"Okay, now back away," Krueger said.

We circled each other in the narrow alley, traded places, him standing next to his car, me backed up against the trashcan near the backdoor. We looked at each other a moment, the sky going a vague orange. The sun was gearing up for morning, light seeping into the world, the color slowly coming back. The chief looked death pale, his hair now completely matted with sweat. I didn't think he'd last long on the run, unless he knew some doctor someplace that maybe owed him a favor.

But it was hard to think beyond the alley and the .32 in the chief's fist.

"You're not talking me back inside to lock me in the cell, are you, Chief?"

He sighed. "No. I guess not."

"You're going to shoot me now."

He nodded. "I like you, Toby. I think you could have grown up and been something. But this is just business. I need to get away as clean as I can, nobody left to answer questions."

I tried to think of some startling piece of logic to convince him to let me live, but I could only think of one word to say.

"Please."

"I'm sorry," Krueger said. "I'll do what I can. I'll make it a clean shot. You want to turn around? Maybe it'll be easier if you don't see it."

And right then it didn't matter how many cowboy movies I'd seen or any cartoon notion I had about being a hero. Right in that moment, I didn't want to see it coming. The image of a bullet coming straight for my nose sent a wave of nausea though me. I was a coward, and I didn't care.

"Okay, wait. L-let me ..." I hated how my voice trembled. "Let me turn around."

"Go on then."

I turned around, and just like that my knees gave out. So light headed. Fear and fatigue and misery pulling me down. I caught myself on the metal trash can, stayed like that for a long moment.

"Wait," I said. "Please. I don't want it in the back. Let me stand up like a man. I can do that at least."

"I understand. Get on your feet."

I pushed myself up, slowly at first.

Then I spun quickly and fired the little green squirt gun.

The ammonia sprayed across his eyes. He yelled pain, fired the revolver, but I'd already ducked underneath and was flying at him for a tackle. It was like throwing myself into a tank, but we went over, me on top, and I had one hand around his gun wrist. With my other hand, I dug a thumb into the bloody bullet hole in the chief's palm.

He screamed, and bucked me off, but he also let go of the revolver.

I grabbed it, stood, backed up three steps. He stood too, cradled his wounded hand. We stared at each other a second, panting.

"All right now," I said, catching my breath. "Let's get you inside and into a cell."

Krueger shook his head. "Nope."

"I'm telling you—"

"Jail's not an option, boy. I won't do it." He came toward me.

"Hold it right there."

"You're going to have to make a decision." He summoned a burst of speed and was on me, his good hand going to my throat.

I strained in his grasp, tried to pull his grip loose with my free hand. "Don't make … me … shoot …" The hand clamped tighter, cutting off oxygen.

"Don't …" I put the gun against his chest.

"You either got the guts for it or you don't, boy. But this is how it ends, one way or another."

Buzzing in my … ears.

My eyesight fuzzed and went dark, mouth opening and closing … trying

… to find.

Air.

Bang.

CHAPTER TWENTY-THREE

When my eyes popped open, I was flat on my back in the alley. I sat up. My throat felt like it was full of hot gravel. The chief lay near me, a hole in the center of his chest. I still clutched the little revolver. I stuck it in my pocket, pushed myself up. My legs felt weak. I was a little dizzy.

Had I been out ten seconds or ten minutes? It didn't matter, I went back inside the station, tossed the .32 on the desk and knelt next to Amanda. She seemed to be breathing normally. Bruises already formed around her throat. I wondered if I'd need Doc Gordon, hoped maybe the phones had come back on by some miracle. I slapped her lightly on the face. It took some coaxing, but she came around.

"You okay?"

She nodded. "I'm a little light headed but I'll live. Where's the chief?"

"In the alley."

"Where are you going?"

I grabbed the shotgun and was already heading for the door. "I've got to do something."

She shouted something after me, but I didn't listen.

I was out to Main Street before she could stop me. I didn't think I really needed the shotgun, but I couldn't imagine going anywhere ever again unarmed. The sun was up. People were out.

Wayne Dobbs tried to stop me as I walked. "What the hell's been going on, Toby? People says there's been gunshots."

"It's over now. Under control." I didn't even slow down.

I met Roy and Howard coming the other way.

"Can I go home yet?"

"Thirty minutes, Roy." I kept walking.

I got to Molly's street, heard the rumble of a big engine, turned back to look.

An old school bus heading out of town. The Mexican illegals hung from the windows, the faces of men, women and children. I saw my smoking buddy. He waved as they went past. I returned the wave but didn't pause.

When I got to Molly's, I let myself in as quietly as I could.

The boy still slept on the couch, a little drool in the corner of his mouth. I wanted to cry he looked so beautiful.

I went into the bathroom, scooped sink water into my mouth, swallowed. It felt cool on my raw throat. There was a little mirror near the sink. Molly probably used it for makeup. I grabbed it and took it back into the living room.

I sat on the floor next to the couch, looked at the boy's face, then at my own in the mirror. I tried to see any hint of me in him. The ears, the nose, the shape of his cheeks, the chin. The color of his hair had been dark when he was first born, but it had gotten lighter each year, with a little strawberry. I looked at myself in the mirror again. Bloodied, bruised and dirty.

"He's been asleep the whole time."

I looked up, saw Molly coming into the room. She'd put on jeans.

"Are you okay?" she asked.

"I think so. It's all over."

"I need to talk to you, Toby."

I stood, set the mirror on the coffee table. "Okay."

"I don't—and please don't be upset—but I don't think we should see each other any more."

"Okay."

"It's just, you know, this stuff with Roy, and the whole night's been crazy, and I'll be heading away for college soon."

"I know. It's okay."

"I really am sorry."

"I don't want you to feel bad about it," I said. "We both knew you'd be going away. Go to college. Get out of this town. Go be something."

A smile tried to invent itself at the corners of her mouth but didn't get very far. "Thanks, Toby."

There would be part of me inside that would be raw and hollow for a while after she left, and I'd get lonely, long for her touch, need to feel her beneath me. But thinking about her leaving wasn't as hard as I thought. It even seemed right, which was a good thing because it was going to happen anyway whether I thought it right or not.

But there was more too. I would miss her when she was gone, but it would be a relief too.

"Thank you for watching TJ. I didn't have anyone else."

"He was good. He slept."

"Thanks."

I bent and scooped up the boy. I held him against my chest with one arm, and he nuzzled his head under my chin, murmuring and drowsy. With the other hand I grabbed the shotgun.

"Roy will be back soon," I told her. "But I think he knows to leave you alone. Just stay out of each other's way until you go to college."

"Don't worry."

"Goodbye, Molly."

"Goodbye, Toby."

And I thought maybe I should kiss her on the cheek or something, but I didn't.

I walked out and didn't know where I was going. My Nova was flipped and it was too far to walk back to my trailer. I headed for the stationhouse.

Coming down Main Street I saw the lights. Two State Police squad cars—no, three. They parked behind and alongside the Jordans' pickup trucks, the blues and reds going crazy, the street filling with citizens who couldn't help but take a look. It had all been too much for the little town, like some bloody carnival act. Everybody wanted a peek at the show.

There would be hard questions. Accusations and blame. But the boy was safe, and I was alive. I'd come though the long night.

I cradled the boy, put the shotgun on my shoulder and walked toward the lights.

My boy was safe. My son.

Mine.

And God help any man who said different.

ONE YEAR LATER

EPILOGUE

I walked into the stationhouse, passed Amanda at the front desk. Another long night shift almost over.

"I need to speak with you, Toby."

"Sure. Can I get some coffee first?"

"No problem."

I went into the back room, poured a fresh cup from the expensive new silver coffee maker. It had a timer on it, and I always set the thing to finish up about five minutes before I walked in, so the stuff would be fresh. I bought the coffee maker out of my first paycheck after they put me on full time. Good coffee too. Columbian.

I filled my mug, went back to the front desk and flopped into the chair opposite Amanda.

"How was it out there tonight?" she asked, not looking up from her stack of paperwork.

"Caught some kids parking and told them to go home."

"A regular crime wave. Anything else?"

"Slow," I said.

"Good. Mrs. Carmichael called in a complaint again about dogs getting into her trash cans. Keep an eye out for strays, okay?"

"Right." We got that complaint from somebody about twice a month. I supposed I'd do what I always did. Not a damn thing.

"How's that Indian woman working out?"

"Alice. Good," I said. "The boy likes her, and her schedule is pretty flexible. I pay her okay."

"Sounds like it's working out."

"It is."

Since that long bad night, Molly had gone off to college. In San Francisco, it turns out. I got exactly one letter from her, saying how great it was and that I should come visit. I didn't answer that letter and didn't get any more. From Doris I'd not heard one peep. Nothing. God help her if she suddenly felt maternal and came back for the boy. Just let her try.

The Jordan Brothers were all buried together on a Saturday, dowager Antonia looking regal in black. The funeral was crowded. The last bit of hurrah for the biggest thing that had happened to the town in decades. Not big in a good way, but it made an impact, and people wanted to be part of it in some way.

People are strange.

Antonia lived three more months and died in her sleep. Maybe she didn't have anything left to live for.

I got a courtesy call that autumn from the warden of the prison where they kept Brett, the oldest Jordan brother. There'd been talk around the yard about how he was going to pay me back times ten when he got out of stir. I thanked the warden for the heads up. Just another little something to worry about in three to five years.

I never saw one of the illegal Mexicans again. They'd promised to get far away, and they'd kept that promise.

I sipped coffee and tried not to get lost in past history.

"Thought I'd tell you we're putting on two new deputies in a week," Amanda said.

One of my eyebrows went up. "Oh?"

"Took forever and a day to get all the paperwork through, and then it took even longer to find acceptable people willing to move out here to the middle of nowhere. This isn't exactly America's fastest growing metropolis. But we managed to find a couple decent candidates."

"Well. That's good then." We'd been stretched pretty thin.

"I need to tell you something else. I'm quitting effective the end of the month."

I stopped sipping coffee, put the mug on the desk. "What?"

"I got a job offer in Idaho," Amanda said. "In one of the ski resort towns. I thought I'd work on my snowboarding."

"Congratulations."

"I'm recommending you for Chief of Police."

I laughed. Hard.

The last year had not been all pleasant. There had been inquiries. The town bloodbath had made the papers in Stillwater and Tulsa. Various insurance companies did not like me. But I had uncovered smugglers and a corrupt police chief. I had been put onto the force full time, a situation which I took as a vote of confidence, although the fact there was nobody else immediately available to do the job was no small part of the decision. There were still a few pending questions (mostly from insurance adjusters) but it looked like there was light at the end of the tunnel.

But Chief of Police? I just couldn't swallow it. I told Amanda as much.

"Think about it," she said. "These new guys don't know the town. Don't know the people. The town council can appoint you Chief of Police. If you want to be Sheriff too, you'll have to go get those votes yourself. But you grew up around here. You've earned some respect."

Maybe. I wanted to believe her. I wanted to think the folks in this town would trust me to do a good job.

"Anyway, my recommendation doesn't mean it's a done deal. But just think about it. That coffee smells good."

"Help yourself."

"Thanks. I think I will." She went into the back room.

I leaned back in the chair, closed my eyes and sipped coffee. It tasted fine. I replayed the events of that night from a year ago, saw it in my head like a little movie. Me and The chief in that alley. His hand on my throat, the gun against his chest. I shivered just thinking about it. How close a thing it had been. I can almost remember pulling the trigger, or maybe I can only imagine it. I'd been a little fuzzy in the head.

But I'd killed him.

The chief was dead.

Long live the chief.

VICTOR GISCHLER is a world traveler, self-proclaimed chicken wing afficianado, Edgar and Anthony Award nominee, Pisces and masked do-badder. His work has been translated into French, Italian, Spanish, German and Japanese. He does not know karate, so feel free to push him down and take his wallet. He earned his Ph.D. in English at the University of Southern Mississippi where they fed him raw liver and beat him with rolled up news-papers. He lives in Baton Rouge with his wife and son.